Flight

Published simultaneously in Canada
Printed in the United States of America

FIRST EDITION

Library of Congress Cataloging-in-Publication Data
Alexie, Sherman, 1966–
    Flight : a novel / Sherman Alexie.
        p.   cm.
    ISBN-10: 0-8021-7037-4
    ISBN-13: 978-0-8021-7037-8
    1. Indians of North America—Fiction.   2. Foster children—Fiction.
I. Title.
PS3551.L35774F57 2007
813'.54—dc22

                                                        2006052656

Black Cat
a paperback original imprint of Grove/Atlantic, Inc.
841 Broadway
New York, NY 10003

Distributed by Publishers Group West

www.groveatlantic.com

07 08 09 10 11 12   10 9 8 7 6 5 4 3 2 1

To Diane

"Po-tee-weet?"

—Kurt Vonnegut,
Slaughterhouse-Five

One

Call me Zits.

Everybody calls me Zits.

That's not my real name, of course. My real name isn't important.

This morning, I wake in a room I do not recognize. I often wake in strange rooms. It's what I do. The alarm clock beeps at me. I know I didn't set that thing. I always set alarm clocks to play wake-up music. Something good like the White Stripes or PJ Harvey or Yeah Yeah Yeahs or Kanye West. Something to start your brain, cook your guts, and get you angry and horny at the same time. Sometimes I wake to my mother's favorite music, like Marvin Gaye or Blood, Sweat & Tears.

Yes, there used to be a band called Blood, Sweat & Tears.

"Hundreds of men, right?"

"Probably."

"Thousands in Seattle, thousands in other cities, hundreds of thousands in the country."

"So what?"

"So what do you think it means for you?"

She stared at me with sympathy. I hate sympathy.

"This is bullshit," I said.

"What is bullshit?" she said.

I laughed at her. I hate it when social workers curse to prove how connected they are to youth and street culture.

"You're a fucking dreamer," I said to her. "What do you think this is, the nineteen-fifties or something? Do you really think I'd become some kind of asshole citizen if I wore a tie and shiny shoes?"

"It would help," she said.

"Whatever."

She leaned close to me. She smelled like cigarettes and cinnamon gum.

"Here's the thing," she said. "You've never learned how to be a fully realized human being."

Jesus, what kind of overeducated bitch says that to a kid?

She made me sound like I was raised by wolves when, in fact, I haven't been raised by anybody.

No, that's not true.

I've been partially raised by too many people.

I've lived in twenty different foster homes and attended twenty-two different schools. I own only two pairs of pants and three shirts and four pairs of underwear and one baseball hat and three pairs of socks and three paperback novels (*Grapes of Wrath, Winter in the Blood,* and *The Dead Zone*) and the photographs of my mother and father.

My entire life fits into one small backpack.

I don't know any other Native Americans, except the homeless Indians who wander around downtown Seattle. I like to run away from my foster homes and get drunk with those street Indians. Yeah, I'm a drunk, just like my father. I'm a good drunk, too. Gifted, you might say. I can outdrink any of those homeless Indians and remain on my feet and still tell my stories. Those street Indians enjoy my company. I'm good at begging. I make good coin and buy whiskey and beer for all of us to drink.

Of course, those wandering Indians are not the only Indians in the world, but they're the only ones who pay attention to me.

The rich and educated Indians don't give a shit about me. They pretend I don't exist. They say, *The drunken Indian is just a racist cartoon.* They say, *The lonely Indian is just a ghost in a ghost story.*

I wish I could learn how to hate those rich Indians. I wish I could ignore them. But I want them to pay attention to me. I want everybody to pay attention to me.

So I shoplift candy and food and magazines and cigarettes and books and CDs and anything that can fit in my pockets. The police always catch me and put me in juvenile jail.

I get into arguments and fistfights with everybody.

I get so angry that I go blind and deaf and mute.

I like to start fires. And I'm ashamed that I'm a fire starter.

I'm ashamed of everything, and I'm ashamed of being ashamed.

This morning, as I count my zits in the mirror, I'm ashamed that I can't remember the names of my new foster mother and father.

I've only been living here in this strange house, with its strange pink bathroom, for two days.

I can't remember the names of my new foster parents' two real kids, either, or the names of the other five foster kids.

When it comes to foster parents, there are only two kinds: the good but messy people who are trying to help kids or the absolute welfare vultures who like to cash government checks every month.

It's easy to tell what kind of people my latest foster parents are. Their real kids have new shoes; the foster kids are wearing crap shoes.

But who cares, right? It's not like I'm going to be here much longer. I'm never in any one place long enough to care.

There's this law called the Indian Child Welfare Act that's supposed to protect half-breed orphans like me. I'm only supposed to be placed with Indian foster parents and families. But I'm not an official Indian. My Indian daddy gave me his looks, but he was never legally established as my father.

Since I'm not a legal Indian, the government can put me wherever they want. So they put me with anybody who will take me. Mostly they're white people. I suppose that makes sense. I am half white. And it's not like any of this makes any difference. I've had two Indian foster fathers, and they were bigger jerks than any of my eighteen white foster fathers.

Of course, I assumed those Indian men would automatically be better fathers to me than any white guy, but I was wrong.

I had this one Indian foster daddy, Edgar, who was great at the beginning. He was a jock, a muscular machine. He took me to Seahawks games. We played touch football and one-on-one hoops in the park. He bought me books.

One time, he gave me this amazing remote control airplane, an F-15 fighter jet. I loved that thing. It was the most amazing gift I'd ever received. It must have cost three hundred dollars. Edgar bought one for himself, too, and we drove out to this remote airplane field in the Cascade Mountain foothills.

"I've been racing planes for years," Edgar said. "So don't take it too hard if you lose, okay?"

"Okay," I said, but I didn't plan on losing.

We piloted our planes around this circular course marked by flags and landed them on a grassy runway.

"Whatever," I say again.

The other kids, the real and the fake ones, all stare at me. It's a riot of cold blue eyes. Those kids know what I'm doing. Some of them already hate me for being a jerk. The rest of them are bored. They've seen it all before.

"Good morning," the foster father says again.

He's challenging me. He thinks he's stronger than I am. He's bigger and taller and older, sure, and has a million more muscles than I do, but I am stronger. I am stronger than all of my fathers.

"What . . . ever," I say, for the third time.

And I say it slow and hard and mean, like each letter was a cussword. And I don't mean the little cusswords like *dick* and *shit*. I mean the big ones like *cock* and *cunt* and *motherfucker*. I think it's strange how curse words frighten and disgust some people. Yes, there are people afraid of certain combinations of vowels and consonants. Isn't that hilarious? Don't those wimps realize that each and every word only has the power and meaning you assign to it? If I decided that *plop* was a dirty word, and started using it to curse people, and convinced enough people to use it as a curse word also, it would eventually become an obscenity.

"Hey," the foster father says. "Look at me."

He's one hundred and eighty-five pounds of blood, and I want to punch him in the carotid artery.

"Don't you look at me that way," he says. "Don't try to stare me down."

Of course, I keep staring at him.

"Stop staring at me," he says.

"Plop," I say.

"What did you say?"

"Plopping plop."

Jesus, I sound like a pissed-off Dr. Seuss character. That thought makes me laugh.

"Are you laughing at me?" he asks.

"You bet your plopping ass I'm laughing at you," I say. I know he wants to punch me.

"I'm going to say good morning one more time," he says. "And if you don't return the favor, you don't get to eat breakfast."

Yeah, like that's a real threat. Yeah, like I haven't been hungry before. Yeah, like I care.

"Good morning," the foster father says.

"Fuck you," I say.

I laugh hard.

"What's so funny?" he asks.

"You're one of them fucking Christians, aren't you?" I ask. Those bastards are always trying to save me, a poor Injun heathen. "Are you going to give me a ticket to Heaven?" I ask.

And now this pretty white boy laughs hard. "Beware of the man whose God is in the skies," he says.

"What does that mean?"

"George Bernard Shaw wrote it."

"So what?"

"So it means I'm not Christian," he says. "I hate Christians. I hate Muslims and Jews and Buddhists. I hate all organized religions and all disorganized ones, too."

"That's a lot of hate," I say.

"I suppose. But hate can be empowering."

"That's a big word."

"You don't know what it means, do you."

"I know what it means."

"Tell me, then."

This guy probably thinks I'm just another stupid street kid. A dyslexic drone in the social welfare system. But I'm smart. Really smart.

Well, okay, maybe not *that* smart. I am currently sitting in a jail cell.

People go to jail for a reason. Well, for a couple of reasons. They're in jail because they're stupid enough to commit crimes. And because they're stupid enough to get caught. And so, yeah, maybe I'm smart but I'm also double-stuff stupid. Adults are always telling me I don't live up to my potential.

I say, fuck potential and anybody who says that fucking word to me.

"You sound like a teacher," I say to the pretty white boy. "Or a preacher."

"And you sound like a child," he says.

"What are you, my grandfather?"

"I'm wise for my age," he says, and laughs, like he's making fun of himself, like people have described him that way before and he thinks it's goofy.

"How old are you?" I ask.

"Seventeen. How old are you?"

"Fifteen."

"All right, Mr. Fifteen," he says. "Tell me what it means to be empowered."

All of a sudden, I feel the need to impress this kid. I want him to like me. More than that, I want him to admire me.

"Empowered means you feel powerful," I say.

"Well, yes, that's obvious," he says. "But how do you obtain that feeling of power? And what do you do with your power after you've found it?"

"I don't know," I say.

He smiles. I can see all thirty-two of his teeth.

"I can show you," he says.

"Hey," he says.

"Hey," I say.

"Aren't you getting tired of spending all your time in jail?"

"Jail here, jail there, it's all the same."

"You're too young to be talking like that," he says.

"Whatever," I say.

Dave shakes his head. He looks disappointed. Depressed, even. I figure he's going to walk away and never return.

"You're running out of chances," he says.

"What chances?" I ask.

"The chance to change your life."

"Whatever," I say.

"Well, listen up, Mr. Whatever," Dave says. "I got you one more chance. Instead of more jail, I talked the judge into sending you to a halfway house."

"Halfway to where?" I ask.

Officer Dave laughs and leaves me to my jailers. And those dang bullies take me out of my cell and ship me to a halfway house for juvenile offenders. I hate group homes even more than I hate foster homes.

I've had some nasty counselors and supervisors in group homes. Mean people, ugly people, and those sick bastards, those Uncle Creepy types, who try to stick their hands down your pants. I got sent to jail once because I punched one of those pedophiles in the crotch. I wanted to break his dick in half.

So I'm lying awake in a ground-floor bedroom of

this juvie halfway house, where all the counselors are Uncle Creepy types who want to give you candy, and I'm thinking about running away when there's a knock on the window.

I pull back the curtains and see him, the beautiful white kid, my new best friend.

I don't know how he found me. But there he is. My hero.

He smiles and breaks the window.

I climb out and we escape together.

We run to an abandoned warehouse in SoDo, an industrial section of Seattle down near the waterfront.

We climb the dangerous stairs to the top floor where the white kid has made a home out of garbage and abandoned office furniture. We sit on chairs made out of newspapers. I laugh.

"What's so funny?" he asks.

"I don't even know your name," I say.

He smiles, walks over to the corner, pulls something out of a sack, and walks back to me.

"This is my name," he says, and hands me two pistols. One of them looks like a regular gun and the other one looks like a Star Wars laser.

"That one is a thirty-eight special," the pretty boy says, "and the other one is a paint gun."

I've seen paint-gun competitions on ESPN, those fake fights where fat white guys run around fake battlefields and shoot each other with balls of Day-Glo dye.

They like to fight fake wars because there aren't enough real ones.

I've seen real people get shot by real guns. But I've never held a real gun. I've always heard and read that guns are cold metal. But not this one. It feels warm and comfortable, like a leather recliner sitting in front of a sixty-inch HDTV.

I laugh again.

"What's funny this time?" he asks.

"Your name is Guns," I say. "That's a really stupid name."

It's his turn to laugh. "My name isn't Guns," he says. "My name is Justice."

We laugh together.

"That is a corny-ass name," I say. "Where'd you get it?"

"I gave it to myself," he says. "But I wish I'd been given my name by Indians. You guys used to give out names because people earned them. Because they did something amazing. And it was the old people who gave out those names: the elders, the wise ones. I wish the wise ones were still here."

I think of the great Oglala Sioux warrior Crazy Horse, who was given his name after he battled heroically against other Indians.

Yes, Indians have always loved to kill other Indians. Isn't that twisted?

I think of how Crazy Horse was speared in the stomach by a U.S. Cavalry soldier while his best friend, Little

Big Man, held his arms. I think of the millions of dead and dying Indians.

"Do you know about the Ghost Dance?" I ask.

"No," Justice says. "Teach me."

"It was this ceremony created by the Paiute holy man Wovoka, back in the eighteen-seventies. He said, if the Indians danced this dance long enough, all the dead Indians would return and the white people would disappear."

"Sounds like my kind of dance," Justice said.

"Yeah, but it didn't work. All the Ghost Dancers were slaughtered."

"Maybe they didn't have the right kind of music."

"Yeah, they should have had Metallica."

Justice and I laugh. And then he stops laughing.

"Did you ever try to Ghost-Dance?" he asks.

"Nobody's Ghost-Danced in over a hundred years," I say. "And I don't think one person can do it well enough to make it work. I think you need all Indians to do it."

"Well, I think you're strong enough to Ghost-Dance all by yourself. I think you can bring back all the Indians and disappear all the white people."

I want to tell Justice that the only Indian I want to bring back is my father and the only white people I want to disappear are my evil foster families.

I guess Justice doesn't realize that a successful Ghost Dance would make him disappear, too. But maybe he doesn't think he's white. Or maybe he thinks he's invincible.

paint gun, Justice asks, "What would you do if the Ghost Dance is real?"

His question echoes in my head. It stays there and I want to give Justice the best answer. The only answer. The answer he wants.

"What if the Ghost Dance is real?" Justice asks me again and again.

The question crawls into my clothes and pushes its way through my skin and into my stomach. The question feeds me.

"Do you think the Ghost Dance is real?" Justice asks.

After hearing that question a thousand times, I finally have the answer.

"Yes," I say.

Justice laughs and hugs me. I am so proud. I feel like I finally deserve his love.

"Okay, okay," he says. "Now you can dance. Now you understand. Now you have the knowledge. Now you have the power. So what are you going to do with that power?"

I stare at the pistol in my hand.

"I'm going to start a fire," I say.

"Yes," Justice says, and keeps on hugging me. He loves me. And I love Justice.

The next day, during lunch hour, I stand in the lobby of a bank in downtown Seattle. Fifty or sixty people are here with me: men, women, and children of many different colors. I hear four or five different languages

being spoken. And I guess these people have many different religions. But none of that matters. I know these
people must die so my mother and father can return.

I breathe, try to relax, and pull the real and paint pistols out of my pocket. I say a little prayer and dance
through the lobby. I aim my pistols at the faces of these
strangers. They scream or fall to the floor or run or
freeze or weep or curse or close their eyes.

One man points at me.

"You're not real," he says.

What a strange thing to say to a boy with a gun. But
then I wonder if he's right. Maybe I'm not real. And if
I'm not real, none of these people are real. Maybe all
of us are ghosts.

Can a ghost kill another ghost?

I push the real and paint pistols into the man's face.
And I pull the triggers.

I spin in circles and shoot and shoot and shoot. I keep
pulling the triggers until the bank guard shoots me in
the back of the head. I am still alive when I start to fall,
but I die before I hit the floor.

Four

"Wake up, kid; come on, it's time to go."

I open my eyes. I'm lying in a hospital bed. No. I'm in a motel-room bed, a small and cheap and filthy motel room. A room where a million ugly people have done a million ugly things. There are stains on the walls, and you don't even want to guess what caused them.

Why am I in this horrible motel room? Well, I did one of the ugliest things a person can do, right? I just shot up a bank full of people. How could I have done that? I think about that man who didn't think I was real. Maybe I wasn't real. Maybe none of it happened. I pray to God that it didn't happen.

But I remember the bank so clearly. I can hear the screams and smell the gunpowder. No nightmare can feel that real, can it?

I want to vomit.

I once read that twenty or thirty people jump off Seattle's Aurora Avenue Bridge every year. And I'm sure that all of them probably changed their minds about suicide the moment after they jumped. Let me tell you, I feel like one of those jumpers. I feel like I jumped off some kind of bridge and changed my mind too late to save any of us.

But why am I alive? Did I really survive a bullet to the brain?

"Damn it, kid," a man says. "Get up, we only have a few minutes."

I don't recognize the man's voice. I sit up in bed and see him sitting on the other bed. He puts on his shoes. He's a serious white guy, maybe forty years old, wearing a blue shirt and blue jeans. He's fat but strong-looking at the same time, like a professional wrestler.

He's also got a pistol in the holster on his belt.

A cop.

I'm not dead, but I am under arrest. But how could I not be dead? I felt that bullet crash through my brain. I saw white light. And then it went dark. And I don't mean asleep dark. I mean shot-in-the-brain-until-you're-dead dark.

But I guess they saved me. Some amazing doctors and nurses must have saved me. They saved the life of a killer. I wonder if it makes them mad or sad when they do that. I wonder if I deserve to live. What the hell was I thinking? What kind of bastard am I? I'm just another zit-faced freak with a gun. Man, I had no idea I was this evil. And then it makes me wonder. Do evil people *know* they're evil? Or do they just think they're doing the right thing?

I think about Justice. I think he fooled me. I think he brainwashed me. If he was so righteous, why wasn't he in the bank with me?

He's free and I'm trapped.

That bullet must have done some major damage. I hope I still have a face and complete skull. I reach up to touch the bandages. But there are no bandages. And there's no blood or scars or any other disgusting head-wound shit. I don't feel any pain at all. In fact, I feel stronger than ever before.

I don't understand what has happened. I survived a bullet to the brain. And I'm in a motel room with a cop.

"Where am I?" I ask the cop.

"We'll both be in a shit storm if we miss this meeting. We fell asleep. Come on. Get up, get your stuff, and let's go."

"Where are we going?"

"Jeez, Hank, shake the sleep out of your brain and get moving."

Hank? Did he just call me Hank?

"My name isn't Hank," I say.

"Quit fooling around, Hank, you're getting me mad."

"Quit calling me Hank."

The cop stands and walks over to me. He leans over me and stares hard at me. His breath smells like beer and onions.

Yes, I've had quite a few ugly smelly guys lean over my bed. I get the urge to punch this cop in the crotch.

"Are you still asleep?" he asks.

"No."

"You're in one of them waking dreams, aren't you?" he asks. "Like sleepwalking or something, right?"

He slaps my cheek lightly. Then slaps me harder.

"Did that help, Hank?" he asks.

"You call me Hank one more time," I say, "and I'm going to kick your ass."

He laughs, pulls me off the bed and to my feet, and shoves me across the room. I trip over a pair of shoes and bump the back of my head against a mirror.

"That's police brutality!" I shout.

The cop just laughs. I've always been good at making cops laugh. But I'm not trying to be funny this time.

"I just got shot in the brain," I say. "Are you trying to kill me?"

He laughs again, grabs a holstered pistol off the table, and hands it to me.

"Okay, soldier up, funny guy," he says. "We got real work to do."

I am stunned. I am the psycho teen who shot up a bank filled with people and a cop just handed me a gigantic freakin' *gun!* A .357 *Magnum!* At least, I think it's a Magnum. I don't know guns much, but I've seen this one in the movies.

I turn around to look at myself in the mirror. I expect to see me pretending to be Clint Eastwood. But instead I am looking at a face that is not my own.

Huh. Isn't that something?

They must have done plastic surgery on me. That bullet must have taken off my face. And so they had to take my zitty teenage Indian mug and replace it with a handsome white guy's face.

Yes, I am looking at a very handsome white guy in the mirror. His hair is blond. His eyes are blue. His skin is clear. This guy hasn't had a zit in his whole life. And this guy is me.

Isn't modern medicine amazing?

"Wow," I say to the cop. "I really like my new face."

He just stares at me.

"It's like that movie with John Travolta," I say. "The one where he switches faces with Nicolas Cage. I didn't know that stuff was real."

The cop's face changes expression. All of a sudden he looks a little confused. And worried. "Did you have a stroke or something, Hank?" he asks. "You're not talking or looking right."

I can't figure out why he keeps calling me *Hank*. Well, maybe they changed my face *and* my name. And so I look down and realize I am shorter than I used to be. In fact, I realize I'm about six or seven inches shorter than I used to be. I'm a short guy now, but I have a lot more muscles. My arms are huge. I have the face and body of a bodybuilder white guy. I am beautiful.

Jeez, I should get shot in the brain every day.

I suddenly get an idea. I reach down and check the size of my groinal region, and I realize that I'm different down there, too. I am a big guy in all sorts of ways.

"Are you sure you're okay?" the cop asks me. "I'm calling this off if you're not okay. It's too dangerous if you're not okay."

"No, no, no," I say. "Everything is good."

Of course, I'm lying. I don't know that everything is good. I am very confused.

"Tell me you're okay," the cop says. "We're not leaving this room unless you say you're okay."

"I'm okay," I say.

He believes me.

"Good. Good, partner, let's go kick some butt," the cop says, and tosses me a wallet. My wallet. I open it up and see a gold badge. My badge. And then I pull an ID card out of the wallet and look at the photo. It's me.

Well, it's a picture of a guy with my new white face. But that ID says that this face belongs to a guy named Hank Storm, and that he's thirty-five years old, and that he's an FBI agent. Yep, a federal agent. A supercop.

"I'm Hank Storm?" I ask the other cop, who must be an FBI guy, too.

"Yes," he says. "You're finally awake. Jeez, Hank, you really had me worried there. All right, let's go save the world."

I put on my shoes and follow him out the door.

Five

The other FBI dude and I step out of our motel room. It's dark and clear and I can see stars in the sky. More stars than I've ever seen. I also see a sign that says this is the Red River Motor Inn.

Red River, Red River, Red River; that name is so familiar. I think I read about it somewhere. And then I remember. Red River is on the Nannapush Indian Reservation.

"Red River, Idaho," I say.

"Yep," the other FBI says. "The asshole of America."

"Lot of Indians here."

"Yeah. I wish Custer would have killed a few more of these damn tepee creepers."

"Wow," I say. "You really hate Indians, don't you?"

"I didn't know any Indians until they sent me to work here. And then I met Indians. And trust me, none of them is worth much. Well, maybe some of the kids. Some of the kids are still okay. But they're going to go bad, too. Just you watch. There's something bad inside these Indians. They can't help themselves."

I wonder what this racist FBI man would do if he knew his partner was really a half-breed Indian. I want to tell him, but I don't want to get punched. Or shot in the head. Again.

So I keep quiet. As quiet as this reservation.

I look at the map inside my memory and realize I'm six hundred miles from the nearest real city. And there are so many stars. I know city lights but I don't know stars.

"The sky is beautiful," I say. "Like a starry blanket."

The other FBI laughs and laughs. "Jeez," he says. "You go to sleep a killer and you wake up like some kind of poet."

"I'm a killer poet," I say.

The other FBI loves that. He slaps me hard on the back, but it doesn't hurt at all because I am very muscular.

"What time is it anyway?" I ask.

"Three in the morn," the other FBI says. "We have to hurry."

So we get into the government sedan and the other FBI drives us through a maze of dirt roads to an old shack sitting out the middle of a dark nowhere. It's so dark I can't see more than four or five feet away. It's like being in the belly of a whale.

"I bet you can't get cell phone reception out here," I say.

"What's a cell phone?" the other FBI asks.

It's my turn to laugh.

"Is the FBI too cheap to give cell phones to its agents?" I ask.

"I don't know what you're talking about," he says.

Wow, this guy isn't kidding. He doesn't know about cell phones. I guess he's old-fashioned. I want to ask him if he's heard of electricity.

Then I see headlights coming down the road behind us.

"All right, all right, get your game face on, kid," says the other FBI. "Things could get ugly real quick."

He pulls out his pistol and checks the ammo.

"Are we going to have a gunfight?" I ask.

"Wouldn't be the first time," he says.

So I pull out my pistol and check the ammo. Okay, I think, I have to be in some kind of dream. This can't be real. I cannot be getting ready for a gunfight. I'm excited and scared. And then I realize something.

"Hey," I say to the other FBI. "What's your name?"

He reacts like I just slapped him.

"You're *not* okay, are you?" he asks. I can see big fear in his eyes. That fear doesn't seem fake. It doesn't feel like a dream. The headlights behind us move closer.

"I'm okay," I say. "I just forgot your name."

"You lied to me," he says. "There *is* something wrong with you, isn't there? Jeez, you had one of them strokes, didn't you? Ah, man, we're in trouble."

He looks back at those headlights traveling toward us. There must be seriously dangerous dudes in that car.

"Just tell me your name," I say.

"Art," he says. "My name is Art. You and I have been partners for twelve years."

"That's a long time," I say.

The other car pulls up beside us. I look inside and see two Indian guys. They look familiar. I stare at them. And they stare at me. And then I realize who they are. They're activists from IRON, which is the acronym for Indigenous Rights Now!

"Hey, Art," I say, "those guys are famous."

Art almost gasps and lets out this squeaky whine, like a little girl on a roller coaster.

"The passenger, what's his name?" I ask.

I remember that the members of IRON gave up their birth names because they were "colonial poison" and named themselves after animals.

"Oh, I remember, his name is Horse," I say.

"Yeah," Art says. His voice cracks.

"And the driver, that's Elk," I say.

Art just nods his head. He looks at me bug-eyed.

"Those guys are super famous," I say. "Famous for Indians, at least. I saw them both in this documentary about the civil war in Red River. You know, that's where IRON was protecting traditional Indians from the evil Indian tribal government dudes. What were they called?"

"HAMMER," Art says.

"Yeah, HAMMER," I say. "What was that short for?"

"Nothing, they just call themselves HAMMER."

"Yeah, IRON versus HAMMER. It was like a goddamn monster movie," I say.

Art's eyes are wide like he's looking at a ghost. And he's looking at me, so I guess he *is* looking at a ghost. He looks over at Horse and Elk, the IRON dudes in the other car. They're talking to each other. But we can't hear them through the glass. Everybody has secrets.

"Oh, yeah, man, I remember now," I say. "Those HAMMER guys were killing everybody back then. And then the FBI joined up with HAMMER and started killing people, too. Man, when was that, back in 1975 or 1976?"

"Hank, you are fucking crazy," Art says. "This *is* 1975, and—you and me—we *are* the FBI."

I laugh. But Art is not kidding. He's telling the truth. Oh, my God! Those damn doctors changed my face and body and put me in a time machine. No, wait. I realize the bank guard did kill me when he shot me in the brain. And I did die, and now I'm living in Hell. I've been sent to Hell. And Hell is Red River, Idaho, in 1975.

"Am I in Hell?" I ask.

Art's anger suddenly changes. There's a little bit of water in his eyes. He looks all compassionate.

"Kid," he says, "I'm sorry, but I think your mind just snapped. But you got to hold it together—okay?—just for a little while. I'll get you through this shit, and we'll get you out of here as soon as we can, okay? We'll get you a head doctor, okay?"

"Okay," I say. I wonder if maybe I did survive that bank guard's bullet but it put me into some kind of coma. I hope this is just a coma nightmare.

"Art," I say, "I'm getting a little freaked out here."

My partner's compassion runs away. His eyes get mean.

"I love you, Hank," he says. "I really do. You're my best friend. You and me, man, together we've been partners for twelve years. I respect you for that, okay? I love you for it. But if you screw this up, I'm going to shoot you in the face."

I believe Art does love me. I am his best friend. And despite all that love and friendship, I am convinced that he will kill me if he has to.

Art rolls down his window. Horse rolls down his window. He has a blue feather tied to his long black braid.

"Hey, Art," Horse says.

"Hey," Art says.

"Hey, Hank," Horse says.

He knows me.

The driver, Elk, who has a square face like he's some kind of Indian Frankenstein, doesn't say anything. He just tries to look tough, and he's doing a pretty good job of it. I'm scared of him.

And then I wonder why these two famous Indian guys are having a meeting with us, the white FBI. I thought they hated the FBI. I thought they were fighting *against* the FBI.

And then I realize that Elk and Horse are double agents. They are traitors to IRON.

This is major news. Back in the future, these guys are still heroes. Everybody still thinks they fought *against* the FBI. My heart is beating a punk rock song against my chest.

"You ready to do this?" Elk asks Art.

"Ready steady," Art says.

All four of us get out of the cars.

Then Elk and Horse open their trunk and pull out another Indian guy: a young dude, maybe twenty. His hands are tied behind his back. His mouth is gagged. And his face is bloody and beaten. He's terrified. And then I notice that all the fingers on his right hand are missing. Somebody cut them off.

I think I'm going to die tonight. Again.

"Is this him?" Art asks. "Does he know what we need to know?"

"Yeah," Elk says. "But he won't tell us."

"What's his name?"

"Junior."

"Looks like you tortured poor Junior," Art says.

"Yeah, but we heap primitive Injuns," Elk says. "We don't have fancy interrogation techniques like the F and B and I."

"I don't know anything fancy," Art says. "Take off his gag."

Elk pulls the gag out of Junior's mouth. All of his teeth are smashed and broken. I almost vomit.

"How's he going to talk with a mouth like that?" Art asks.

"Didn't mean to punch him that hard," Horse says.

"You did that much damage with one punch?" Art asks.

"Yeah," Horse says. He's proud. And I do vomit a little bit into my mouth and swallow it back down.

"All right," Art says. "Hold his arms."

Elk and Horse hold Junior's arms. He doesn't fight back.

"All right, Junior," Art says. "Are you going to tell me what I want to know?"

Junior shakes his head.

In my head, I scream, *Tell them, Junior, tell them everything!*

I wish I knew what Art wanted to know. Maybe I could save Junior if I knew.

Art takes out his pistol and presses it against Junior's forehead. Poor Junior barely even reacts. He's already given up.

I look at Elk and Horse. They're smiling. I realize they aren't freedom fighters or anything like that. They don't care about protecting the poor and defenseless. No, man, these guys just like to hurt people. And I look at the weird light in Art's eyes. He isn't a lawman. He doesn't protect our country. He just likes to hurt people, too.

"All right, Junior," Art says. "You get one chance. Tell me what I want to know."

And then Junior, amazing little Junior, he gets this look in his eyes. It's peaceful and defiant at the same time. It's like he's saying, *Kill me if you want. It doesn't matter. I'm still a better person than you.*

"Are you going to talk?" Art asks.

Junior shakes his head.

"Are you going to talk?" Art asks again.

"No," Junior says.

Horse and Elk release Junior's arms and step back. He could run now if he wanted to, but he wouldn't get far.

"Are you going to talk?" Art asks for the third time.

"Fuck you," Junior says.

Art shoots him in the face and Junior drops. He's gone.

"You got blood on me," Elk says to Art.

"We all got blood on us," Art says.

He's right about that.

Art looks at me. I stare back. And then I spin around and vomit all over the place.

Art killed that guy so easily. You don't kill that easily unless you've done it lots of times before. I wonder who taught Art how to shoot people with a real gun.

And all of this just makes me vomit some more.

When I look up, Elk and Horse smirk at me.

"What's wrong with you, FBI?" Elk asks. "It's not like this is your first one."

"What?" I ask.

"Don't play dumb," he says. "I know what you did. I saw you."

Elk smiles. I hate that smile. He *knows* me.

Have I killed somebody out here on the reservation? Why don't I remember it? Maybe Hank Storm killed people. But then I remember the bank. I'm not any better than these men. I'm not any better than the real Hank Storm.

I am Hank Storm, too.

"Don't worry about Hank," Art says. "He isn't himself tonight."

"Yeah," I say. "I am most definitely not the old Hank Storm. I'm a whole different kind of Hank."

"What are we going to do about Junior's body?" Elk asks.

"Let him rot," Art says.

"He's a traditionalist," Elk says. "His soul won't get to Heaven if we don't bury him the Indian way."

"Why do you care?" Art asks.

"Because I was taught to," Elk says. He's thinking hard. Then he surprises me. "Why don't you guys get going," he says. "We'll bury him the right way."

Horse grunts in agreement.

Elk and Horse tortured Junior and delivered him to his murderers. But now they are going to bury him with respect. I don't understand people.

"All right," Art says. "But I need something else first."

"What?" Elk asks.

Art looks hard at me. "Shoot Junior," he says.

"What?" I ask.

"Shoot Junior," Art says again.

"He's already dead."

"Shoot him," Art says and points his gun at me. "Or I'll shoot you."

"I don't understand," I say. "He's already dead. You can't kill him twice."

"I want your bullet in him," Art says. "I want us to be in this one together."

"But that's not respectful, is it?" I ask Elk. "That's not the Indian thing to do, is it?"

"You're not Indian," Elk says.

"Shoot him," Art says. "Now."

Scared, I pull out my pistol and stand over Junior's body. He looks so young. He's a kid. Like me. I aim my gun at his chest. At his heart.

I can't do this. It somehow seems worse to shoot a dead body than to shoot a living man. Justice made killing make sense. But it doesn't make sense, does it?

I'm going crazy. I *am* crazy. I want somebody to tell me that I'm not real.

"Shoot him," Art says.

I close my eyes and pull the trigger.

Maybe you can't kill somebody twice for real, but it sure hurts your heart just the same.

Six

When I open my eyes, I'm in a hospital room. For a moment I wonder if I'm back to being myself, to being Zits, but then I see Art sitting in a chair at the foot of my bed. I'm still trapped inside Hank Storm. But then I wonder if I've always been Hank Storm and was only Zits in a nightmare. Maybe I didn't shoot up that bank full of people. I hope I'm just the man who shot an already dead guy in the face. Jesus, what kind of sick consolation can that be?

"Hey, Hank," Art says. "Welcome back."

"Where have I been?" I ask.

"Asleep."

I just stare at him.

"How you feeling?" he asks.

Fucked by time, I think, and fucked by memory.

"Art," I say, "you have no idea where my brain is right now."

"You're talking about that thing back on the reservation?" Art asks.

Not really, I think, but I might as well talk about that awful shit, too.

"Yeah," I say. "The last thing I remember was standing over that guy, and—"

I can't finish the sentence.

"After you did what I told you to do," Art says, "you passed out."

Can you blame me? I want to get out of bed and run away from Art, but I'm too weak.

"What happened after I passed out?" I ask.

"I thought you'd gone mental," he says, "but it turns out you had some virus."

"I'm sick?"

"Yeah. After you passed out, I shoved you into the car and drove fast. I barely got you to the hospital in time. I thought you were going to die."

I think about Elk and Horse.

"What happened to those two other guys?" I ask.

"I left them there," Art says. "They had stuff to do."

"How long have I been out?" I ask.

"Three days."

"Wow," I say.

"Yeah, the doctors thought you maybe damaged your brain with that fever."

"It's only a virus," I say. "I don't think you can catch what I have."

"Maybe I want to," she says.

I can't believe this woman is my wife. She is beautiful. Black hair, blue eyes, pale skin. She is maybe the most beautiful woman I have ever seen in person.

I wonder if I'll get to have sex with her.

I know this sexy woman is Hank's wife. But I'm Hank right now. And she loves him so she loves me, too. I wonder if she knows that Hank kills people. I wonder if she knows that Hank helped kill a man a few nights ago. I wonder if she would still love Hank if she knew. I suspect she might. I suspect she sees Hank as her protector, as her children's protector.

Hank makes the world safe. He is a good and loving husband and father. He is one hundred different versions of himself, and only one of them is a killer.

"I hear you're coming home," my wife says.

"I think so," I say.

"That's good, we've missed you so much."

She kisses me on the mouth. It makes me feel powerful. I close my eyes again and kiss her back as hard as I can.

God, I think I would kill for her kiss.

Seven

I'm running through the dark. I run toward the sound
of laughter. I run toward a bright light in the distance.

I run super fast. And I wonder if I'm not running at
all. What if I'm flying? What if I have become that bank
guard's bullet? What if I'm the bullet that blasted
through my brain?

But, wait, no, I suddenly burst through the bright
light, which is really the opening of a buffalo-skin tepee,
and I run outside and stop.

I am standing in the middle of a gigantic Indian camp.
And I don't mean some Disneyland, Nickelodeon,
roller-coaster, stuffed-animal, cotton-candy Indian camp.

Nope.

I am standing in the middle of a real Indian camp, complete with thousands of real Indian tepees and tens of thousands of real old-time Indians.

The tepees go on forever. They're grouped in little circles inside bigger circles inside the biggest circles. This camp sits beside a small river. Small dusty hills rise above the water. Thin dry trees cover the hills.

I breathe dust; it makes mud in my mouth.

And there are so many Indians.

Yep, a bunch of real old-time Indians. I'm not exactly sure what year it is. It's tough to tell the difference between seventeenth- and eighteenth- and nineteenth-century Indians.

These are how Indians used to be, how Indians are supposed to be. Justice always talked with admiration about Indians like this.

These old-time Indians have dark skin. There aren't any half-breed pale-beige green-eyed Indians here. Nope, unlike me, these Indians are the real deal.

I don't hear any of them speaking English. I don't know what Indian language they are speaking. I can't understand it, but all of them are speaking it. In fact, as I listen more closely, I realize these Indians—men, women, children, and old people—are speaking a bunch of different languages. So there are a lot of different tribes here.

Even the dogs seem to be barking in Indian. And there are a lot of dogs, hundreds of dogs.

And it stinks something fierce.

There are tens of thousands of human beings living in close quarters in the summer heat. And yes, it has to be summer because the sun is huge in the blue sky and it must be about 120 degrees.

So imagine a camp filled with tens of thousands of sweating Indians, dogs, and horses, along with what appears to be the rotting and drying corpses of hundreds of buffalo, deer, porcupines, badgers, squirrels, rats, and who-knows-what other animals, hanging on racks everywhere I look.

These Indians eat a lot of meat.

And deodorant has not been invented yet.

And it's hotter than the pizza cheese that gets stuck to the roof of your mouth and burns you so bad you can have one of those skin flaps hanging down.

Imagine what this smells like.

Justice never said anything about the smell of old-time Indians. I never read anything about this smell. I never saw a television show that mentioned it.

I don't mean to be disrespectful, but it smells like the Devil dropped a shit right here in the middle of this camp.

But you know what's really crazy? I seem to be the only one bothered by the stench. Everybody else is smiling and gossiping and singing and laughing and living their way-cool old-time Indian lives. None of them are gagging and covering their noses like me.

And then I remember how some people's houses just smell funny. They don't stink. Not really. But they smell different. A few times in my life, I walked into new foster homes and knew I'd never be able to live there because of the strange smell.

Everybody's house smells different. Some of them smell good, most of them just smell different, and a few of them stink.

So this huge village is like one of those stink houses. And the people who live here don't notice the stink.

People smell different, too. Sometimes you meet people and you think they're nice and decent, and it seems like you might be friends. But you get closer to them and they stink. They smell like rotten fish or dead raccoons or something. And you just have to run away.

Later, you mention the bad smell to your other friends and they say they didn't smell anything different. That stink is reserved especially for you.

But, hey, it works the other way, too. Sometimes you meet a person, and you catch the scent and it's like you've smelled a garden in Heaven, because all you want to do is follow that person around and breathe in for the rest of your life.

And later you mention this great scent to your other friends, and they say they didn't smell anything different.

I remember this one time, when I was taking a video class at a special program for homeless kids in Seattle. I was learning how to use a computer to edit movies.

And the teacher—her name was Sue—she smelled exactly like Campbell's vegetable soup.

Now I never thought the smell of Campbell's vegetable soup was sexy. I always liked it, but it didn't get me all hormonal or anything. But when I smelled Sue, I began to think that Campbell's vegetable soup might be the sexiest thing in the world.

Of course, being young and stupid and in love, I told Sue that she smelled exactly like Campbell's vegetable soup. She just laughed at me.

But, wait, why am I talking about soup? Maybe it's just safer and funnier to think about soup and sexy women named Sue than it is to find yourself transported to an old-time Indian camp.

And then I look down at myself and realize that I'm an old-time Indian kid, maybe twelve or thirteen years old. I'm thin and muscular, and the only thing I'm wearing is a loincloth.

I get shy for a second because I'm almost naked. But then I realize that every boy and man in the camp is wearing only a loincloth. And a few of the women and girls are pretty much naked, too.

Then I solve a mystery: I look under my loincloth.

Okay. I know for sure now that Indians didn't have underwear beneath their loincloths.

Then I see this huge Indian guy, like the Arnold Schwarzenegger of Indian warriors, walking toward me. He gets closer and closer. He's fierce. His face and body are war-painted in ten different colors, he's carrying this epic tomahawk, and I get scared. I wonder if he's magic. Maybe he knows I'm not really this old-time Indian boy. Maybe he can feel that I'm just borrowing this body.

I want to run but I'm frozen. Where would I run to anyway? When you're trying to escape from Indians, it's probably best if you don't start your escape from inside their huge camp.

But just when I think the warrior guy is going to chop off my head, he leans over, picks me up, and hugs me tightly. And I realize this is my father.

My father.

Well, okay, he's the father of the kid whose body I'm inside at the moment. But as long as I'm this kid, this man is my father. And since I never knew my real Indian father, I feel like I'm going to explode.

I want to hug this guy forever and forever.

I scream out *Daddy!* But nothing comes out of my mouth. Huh. What happened? I try to scream *Daddy!* again. Nothing.

My father sets me down and then takes my hand and leads me through the camp. I keep trying to scream *Daddy!* but nothing happens.

I reach up, touch my throat, and feel a huge fleshy knot. It's on my voice box. I don't know if I was attacked by a person or by a disease, but my voice has been taken away.

Damn.

But I feel okay. This guy loves me. He's singing to me. Who knew that old-time Indian braves serenaded their sons? It's beautiful. I'm in love.

I wonder if this is Heaven. Maybe God sent me to Hell first. Maybe he made me watch Art kill Junior because I needed to learn from my mistakes.

Maybe I learned something.

Maybe God forgave me and sent me to Heaven.

Maybe this Indian camp is Heaven—a stinky Heaven.

And, okay, maybe God didn't forgive me completely, so he put me in the body of a kid without a voice. But that's okay. I can live without a voice as long as this man, my new father, keeps loving me like he does.

And then I am hit with more love lightning. I bet my new father is carrying me to our family tepee, where my new mother and my new brothers and sisters are waiting for me. I have a family. A real family. A true family.

I am happy for the first time in my life.

Eight

Happiness never lasts long, does it?

As my new father leads me through camp, I realize this cannot be Heaven.

All these old-time Indians are doomed. They're going to die of disease. And they'll be slaughtered by U.S. Cavalry soldiers. They'll be packed into train cars and shipped off to reservations. And they'll starve in winter camps near iced-over rivers.

The children are going to be kidnapped and sent off to boarding schools. Their hair will be cut short and they will be beaten for speaking their tribal languages. They'll be beaten for dancing and singing the old-time Indian songs.

All of them are going to start drinking booze. And their children will drink booze. And their grandchildren and great-grandchildren will drink booze. And one of those great-grandchildren will grow up to be my real father, the one who decided that drinking booze was more important than being my father. The one who abandoned my mother and me.

That's what is going to happen to all these old-time Indians. That's what's going to happen to me. This is what Justice was always talking about. Old-time Indians were so beautiful, and they were destroyed.

It makes me angry. I want to spit and kick and punch and slap. I want to cry and sing, but I cannot use my voice.

And then my father stops to talk to a funny-looking Indian guy. I listen to them talk Indian. I don't know exactly what they're saying, but I do know they're arguing.

This new Indian guy is short, barely taller than I am. And he's very pale, almost white-skinned. In fact, he's got patches of skin peeling off his back, chest, and arms. This Indian is so white he gets sunburned.

His hair isn't black at all. Nope, it's light brown, and some strands of it are almost blond. He's got a single eagle feather tied into his braid and white lightning bolts painted on his body.

Oh, my God! This pale little dude is Crazy Horse, the strange man of the Oglalas!

Yes, this is the famous mystical Indian warrior who killed hundreds of white people. This guy was the greatest warrior ever.

I am looking at Crazy Horse, the magical one. Bullets couldn't hit him. He could never be photographed. He was a holy ghost, the Sioux Jesus. Well, sort of like Jesus. I mean, Jesus didn't kill anybody, you know? So Crazy Horse was like Jesus, if Jesus had been a warrior.

I am standing right next to him. And his eyes are gold-colored.

I think the greatest warrior in Sioux history is a half-breed mystery. I think this legendary killer of white men *is* half white, like me.

I look around again at the Indian camp. Thousands of tepees. Tens of thousands of Indians. Hot summer day. Dusty hills surrounding us. The skinny river close by.

Crazy Horse is here. And that older Indian dude standing over there by the horses? He sure looks like Sitting Bull does in the history-book pictorials.

I realize this skinny river is the Little Bighorn, and I have been transported back to June 1876.

I grab my father's leg and shake him.

I scream, *Daddy! Daddy! This is the camp at the Little Bighorn! Custer is coming! Custer is coming! He's bringing the Seventh Cavalry and they're coming to kill us!* But of course I cannot actually say anything because I don't have a working voice box.

My father stares at me. I don't need to speak his language to know he wants me to shut up, even if I'm not really making any noise.

And then I remember that the Indians at Little Big-horn already know that Custer is—was—coming. In fact, they set up this camp so that Custer would come for them. It's a trap.

George Armstrong Custer and his Seventh Cavalry are marching here. There are only about seven hundred white soldiers riding with Custer. And waiting here in the camp for him are three or four or five thousand Indian warriors. Custer is marching toward his slaughter.

Custer is a crazy egomaniac who thinks he is going to be president of the United States. Custer is one of the top two or three dumb asses in American history.

I can't believe I'm here. This is the Battle of the Little Bighorn. This is Custer's Last Stand. I wonder when it's going to start.

And then I hear gunfire in the distance. We all hear that gunfire. The Indian warriors race for their weapons and their horses.

Thousands of hot and angry Indian dudes ride out to meet Custer and his doomed soldiers.

Nine

They named the battle all wrong.

They shouldn't have called it Custer's Last Stand. Oh, it was his last stand. He died there. Here, I mean. But Custer wasn't important. He was easily replaced. There were plenty of other soldiers who were smarter and better at killing Indians.

Little Bighorn was the last real battle of the Indian Wars. After that, the Indians gave up. So Custer's Last Stand was really the Indians' last stand. But, oh, on that day, this day, the Indians are crazy good. And crazy ready.

I'm not stupid. I don't want to get shot again. I'm only twelve or thirteen years old, and I'm small. So I stay in camp and listen to the sounds of battle.

I can't see anything, but I know what's happening. I read about this fight. I watched a TV show about it on the History Channel.

A few days ago, Custer ignored his superior officer's orders and force-marched his men toward the Little Bighorn. They were only supposed to march twenty miles a day but Custer made them march seventy miles a day.

He was supposed to take his time and not arrive here ahead of the soldiers who were hauling the huge and heavy Gatling guns. Custer decided he didn't need the Gatling guns, those old-time machine guns that blasted one hundred bullets a minute.

What an overconfident asshole, huh?

When Custer arrived on the hills above the Little Bighorn, he was supposed to wait for the other army dudes to show up. A couple thousand more soldiers.

But he didn't wait. He wanted all the glory for himself. So he sent half of his men to attack one side of the Indian camp, and he took the other half and rode toward the opposite end of the camp.

He thought he was going to terrify the Indians and make them run away, but he ran into a few thousand organized Indians—with repeating rifles.

Yep, these particular Indians said, "Fuck bows and arrows. We're going to get technological!"

After meeting the superior numbers of Indians, Custer ordered the retreat. The cavalry rode back up into the hills with the Indians in hot pursuit. But it was too late. It was going to be Custer's last day.

It *is* his last day. I stand in the camp and listen to the battle.

It's all gunfire and screams and Indian singing and silence and more silence and then the sounds of celebration. I swear I hear laughter.

The battle is over. It only takes about an hour. A quick and brutal fight.

So I walk toward the hill where Custer and his soldiers lie dead and dying. I walk with hundreds of other Indians. Women, children, old people.

We walk to join the warrior men. And some warrior women. A lot of women put on war paint and rode out into battle against Custer. I never knew Indian women could be warriors, too.

It's hormonal to say this, but those women warriors are sexy in their war paint.

But there is nothing sexy or beautiful on Custer's Hill. There are hundreds of dead cavalry soldiers. Bloody corpses everywhere. They look like red and white flowers blooming in the green grass.

I feel sick in my stomach and brain. I feel sick in my soul. I remember that in another life I killed people like this. I left behind a bank lobby filled with dead bodies.

But this is war. The Indians were protecting themselves from the soldiers. Custer had ridden into camp to kill men, women, and children. He had to be stopped.

I understand why he's dead. I understand why he had to be killed. It was self-defense. Wasn't it self-defense?

I understand why the soldiers had to be killed, but I don't understand what is happening to the soldiers now. To their bodies.

All around me, Indian men, women, and children are desecrating the bodies of the dead white soldiers.

Right there, an Indian grandmother is stabbing a soldier with his own bayonet. He's dead and bloody, but she keeps stabbing him over and over again.

I stand and watch as she strips off his clothes. She wants him to be naked and ashamed in the afterlife.

And now she cuts off his penis and stuffs it into his mouth. She wants the gods to laugh at him when he arrives in the afterlife. "Hey, kid," the gods will say to him, "do you know you have your own cock stuffed between your teeth?"

All around me, grandmothers are cutting off penises and ears and hands and fingers and feet.

I see a young woman, a girl, maybe ten years old, digging at a dead soldier's eyes. I run over to her and push her away. She's trying to take his eyes.

She shouts at me in her tribal language. I don't know exactly what she's saying, but she's cursing. And then I realize that she thinks *I* want his eyes. She thinks *I'm* fighting for his eyes.

She pushes me. I push her back. She pushes me. I punch her in the face.

And then somebody grabs me. I am being dragged across the grass, up the hill, toward the summit. My father drags me.

I look back and watch that girl cut out the dead soldier's eyes. He'll be blind in the afterlife and he won't be able to find Heaven. Lost and alone, his ghost will wander this battlefield forever.

My father drags me to the summit.

There I see a hundred Indian warriors have surrounded six white soldiers, the only survivors. They are being tortured.

The warriors slap and kick and punch the white soldiers. They toss them to the ground. Then they pick them up and throw them down again. They cut them with arrowheads and knives and hatchets. A thousand little cuts.

This is war.

My father drags me into the circle. The other Indian warriors stop to watch this. Something important is happening. I am somebody important.

My father grabs one of the white soldiers. He's just a kid, like me. I didn't know they let kids join the cavalry.

My father tosses the kid to the ground and steps on him. Holds him down. Then my father takes the long knife out of his belt and hands it to me.

I see the knife is the broken end of a cavalry bayonet. The handle is a thick wrap of beaded buckskin.

My father says something to me in his language. I don't understand.

He says the same thing again. I still don't understand.

He points at me, at my throat. I reach up and touch the huge scar on my neck.

And then I remember: A white soldier cut my throat. In another camp on a different river, a white soldier grabbed my hair, lifted my chin, and slashed my throat with a bayonet. And now my father wants revenge. He wants me to want revenge.

I remember, back when I was Zits, back when I was eight years old, and I was living in this foster home on a mountain near Seattle. A rich white family. I thought their money made me rich, too. They bought me new shoes. It was the first time I ever wore new shoes.

I remember I'd been living there for a week, with my new brother and new sister and new mother, when my new father took me into the basement to show me his model trains. He had miles and miles of railroad track down there. Thousands of miles and hundreds of trains. He had built cities and towns and mountains and forests.

I remember I played with those trains for hours and hours. Played until I could barely keep my eyes open. Then my new father took me into another dark room in the basement, one without any trains, and did evil things to me. Things that hurt. Things that made me bleed.

I stare at the white kid, the soldier, lying on the ground of Little Bighorn. I stare at the bayonet in my hand.

I stare at my Indian father. I notice that he has little hands war-painted on his chest, children's hands. I wonder if he paints himself that way to remember the Indian children who have been destroyed by white soldiers.

I stare at the white soldier again.

I wonder what I would do now if that model-train man were lying on the grass here at Little Bighorn. Would I kill him? Would I take revenge on him for what he did to me in the dark basement room?

I don't know.

All around me, Indian men, women, and children watch me. They all want revenge. They all want me to want revenge.

The other white soldiers, bloody and broken, watch me. They know they are going to die and they weep. They want to live.

Yes, they are soldiers. They are killers. And they want to live.

We all want to live. I don't know what to do.

I feel the anger building inside of me. I feel the need for revenge. Maybe I'm only feeling the old-time Indian kid's need for revenge. Or maybe I'm only feeling *my* need for revenge. Maybe I'm feeling both needs for revenge.

And then I wonder if that's the reason I killed all the people in the bank.

Did I want revenge? Did I blame those strangers for my loneliness? Did they deserve to die because of my loneliness?

Does this little white soldier deserve to die because one of his fellow soldiers slashed my throat?

If I kill him, do I deserve to be killed by this white soldier's family and friends?

Is revenge a circle inside of a circle inside of a circle?

I look away from the white kid's eyes. I look across the distance and see Crazy Horse astride a pony on another hill. He's alone. He's always alone.

He watches us. He is not participating. Yes, he killed dozens of soldiers during this fight. And he killed Custer. But then he rode away to watch the rest of it. Alone.

I remember that he always camped alone. That he often left his people and traveled into the wilderness. I remember that he went missing for weeks and months at a time. Nobody knew where he went.

And now I watch him ride over the hill and disappear.

Soon, he will be killed. Not by a bullet. According to legend, Crazy Horse was bulletproof. Crazy Horse will be murdered by one of his old friends: by Little Big Man.

Another Indian warrior will betray Crazy Horse. Little Big Man will hold Crazy Horse's arms as a white soldier punches a bayonet into the strange one's belly.

A bayonet will kill Crazy Horse. Like the bayonet in my hand.

My father yells at me in his language. He wants me to be a warrior.

I'm only twelve or thirteen. This body is only twelve or thirteen. I am only a child.

I stare at the white soldier in front of me. He's probably eighteen. Or younger. He's seventeen or sixteen or fifteen. He's a child and I'm a child and I'm supposed to slash his throat.

What do I do?

I close my eyes.

Ten

I open my eyes to reveille. Somebody blares away on his trumpet. No, a bugle. The military uses a bugle. What is the difference between a trumpet and a bugle? I try to picture a bugle in my mind. And a trumpet.

The bugle doesn't have valves or keys. The bugle is a naked trumpet. I wonder who plays that bugle.

I get out of bed. No, it's a cot. And I realize I'm in a tent, with maybe ten or twelve other cots. But they're all empty. I'm alone here.

I can hear people running and yelling outside the tent.

Oh, yeah, that's reveille. That means it's morning. Everybody must be up getting breakfast or getting ready to fight. I guess I must be a soldier now. I wonder which war I'm going to be fighting.

I wonder who I might have to kill now. I want this to stop. But what can I do? There must be some way to escape. I have to make something happen. So I walk outside the tent.

One hundred U.S. Cavalry soldiers are rushing around. These are old-time soldiers, nineteenth or eighteenth century, like the soldiers at the Little Bighorn, I think. Jesus, I hope this isn't Custer's Seventh Cavalry.

I need a mirror. I want to look at my reflection to see who I am this time. But then I notice that the other soldiers are looking at me. Some are laughing and pointing. Then all of them are laughing and pointing.

There's something wrong. With me.

I look at myself: I am naked as a bugle.

I guess this guy likes to sleep naked.

I'm embarrassed but also relieved. I am not that kid soldier. Nope. I am an old man, skinny and wrinkly. That's bad enough, but you know what's worse? My pubic hair is gray.

So, okay, I suddenly realize I've been staring at my nakedness for way too long. I look up to see the soldiers laughing even harder at me. So I dash back into my tent. Well, I go as fast as I can. I limp, really. But I limp fast, damn it. I notice that my body is not too responsive to my commands. My legs hurt, especially my knees. I bet I have arthritis; old people get that disease, and I'm old.

So I limp to my cot and look for clothes, my uniform. I find it. I guess it's my uniform. It seems to be

my size. I sniff it. It smells like the old man I am now.
I try to put the thing on, but it has snaps and buttons
and suspenders and belts I don't understand. And my
fingers don't work too well. I have to concentrate on
making them work right. And they hurt. It's like little
knives stabbing my knuckles.

Then I remember that God is really, really old. So
maybe God has God arthritis. And maybe that's why the
world sucks. Maybe God's hands and fingers don't work
as well as they used to.

Maybe God looks down on earth and sees the bad
guys and tries to pick them up. Maybe he wants to
squish them like bugs. But God's arthritis is so bad he
can't make his fingers work.

Maybe God saw me pull out my guns in the bank and
tried to reach down and squish me before I could kill
anybody. But God's hands were too slow. He got me,
but only after I shot a bunch of people.

I'm ashamed of myself. Who was I? Well, I was me.
I don't have any excuses. I shot people. That's all I can
say. I deserve whatever punishment comes my way.

But no punishment will be big enough. My punishment
will not bring back the dead. It doesn't work that way.

I will be punished and the dead will stay dead. And
the world will keep going on like that.

Frustrated, I keep losing my grip as I try to button
my uniform. I am late for reveille. And I'm sure it's bad
to be late for reveille.

So, okay, now I'm dressed and I limp out of the tent to join the other soldiers. Everybody else is already lined up in neat rows—or semi-neat rows, I guess. All of these soldiers are young and hungry. I wonder how long they've been on the march. They're not starving to death, but they look hollow-eyed and barren, like they've been fed just enough food but never enough happiness.

But why am I so worried about their happiness? About their loneliness? I know I'm going to get my ass kicked if I can't figure out where I belong in this formation. But I don't see a sign that says OLD-FART SOLDIERS BELONG HERE.

"Gus!"

I hear somebody shout that name but I don't connect to it, so I keep walking up and down the rows of young soldiers, looking for my place. I'm about to shove some kid aside and take his place in line. I already hate these little shits. They're still laughing and insulting me with quiet voices. They snicker.

Are soldiers allowed to snicker? I thought military training gets rid of snickering.

This feels like a nomadic high school in the middle of the Old West. These guys are soldiers, sure, and they might be good soldiers. But they're still just kids, cruel and impulsive.

It reminds me of the time when I was twelve years old, and this rich Seattle dude decided to start a charity for disadvantaged youth. He was going to take us homeless and pointless kids on "educational journeys" all over the world.

The rich guy's motto: "How can you be a part of the world if you haven't seen the world?"

My motto: "I don't need to see the world in order to know the world is filled with homeless and pointless kids."

Each day, worldwide, twelve thousand children starve to death. *That* is fucked up.

So, anyway, this rich guy picked twelve of us Seattle kids and we went to New York City. It was fun, I guess. We stayed in a fancy hotel and went to museums and Broadway plays and the Statue of Liberty. But it was at Newark Airport where I received a real education.

At the baggage claim, I saw a bunch of army soldiers waiting for their baggage. Three or four soldiers grabbed another soldier's bag and played keep-away with it. They were all dressed in their best uniforms with all their little medals and ribbons, and they were playing keep-away from this nerd soldier, who was wearing thick black army glasses and had big old army-nerd zits on his face. His zits were worse than mine.

Yeah, sure, these guys were serving their country, and a few of them might become big-time heroes, but they were just kids, all eighteen or nineteen years old: immature and goofy and mean and acne-scarred and funny and stupid and silly and unsure about everything.

And these are the children we send to fight our wars. I'm the child that Justice sent to war. And all of us children fight to defend adults. Doesn't that seem backward?

"Gus! You deaf dusty bastard! Get up here!"

Somebody is yelling at me. I guess my name is Gus. Stupid name, really. But who am I to judge? I'm a time-traveling mass murderer and my name is Zits.

"Gus!" the guy shouts again. He's a little general dude with a mustache that probably weighs more than he does. "Have you gone mad? Please, sir, get up here now."

"All right, all right," I say, and I notice that I'm speaking with this weird accent, like I'm Irish or something. Maybe I am finally Irish. Gus doesn't sound like an Irish name, but Zits isn't exactly a highly sacred Indian name, either.

"Okay, troops," General Mustache shouts to the assembled children, "I want you to meet Augustus Sullivan. You can call him Gus. He's the best Indian tracker in the entire U.S. Army."

Oh, shit! I'm in the body of a guy who hunts Indians. God is definitely one funny deity-dude.

"I want you all to take a good hard look at Gus," General Mustache says. "He's an old man, and you might think he's weak and useless, but this is the bravest, strongest man I have ever known. I have fought alongside him for twenty years. I believe in him. I trust him. I would follow him anywhere."

I guess I am some kind of hero.

"Two months ago, in Kansas," General Mustache continues, "a group of settlers was attacked by wild Indians. They were all slaughtered: men, women, and children. Whole families. Those savages murdered twenty-five Christian folks. And Gus here, all on his own, went looking for the Indians who did it. And he found their camp on the Colorado River and he's going to lead us there. And we are going to deliver unto them the swift and deadly blow of justice."

Okay, so this is not good. I am supposed to lead one hundred white soldiers into an Indian village.

I can't do it.

I'm in control of Gus now so I'm just going to lead all these soldiers away from the Indian village. That might be a little difficult, I suppose, since I have no idea where the village is. I don't even know north from south. But my lack of direction will probably be a good thing. I don't need to get lost on purpose.

So that's my plan. I'm just going to get on my horse, point it in a random direction, and get very, very lost.

Of course, when you're a time-traveling mass murderer, you can't really expect things to work out as planned. If there are rules for time travelers, I don't know them.

But things are not just happening. None of this is random.

You see, I try to get lost. I try to lead the soldiers astray. But it doesn't work that way.

Some part of the old Gus remains inside of me. I still have Gus's abilities. Whenever I zig, Gus makes me zag and so, zigzagging through the trees and grass and hills, we make our way toward the Indian camp. And even though I keep thinking, *I want to be lost, I want to be lost, I want to be lost,* I can't do it. Gus won't let me. What it comes to is this: I can't completely control Gus. I can move his arms and legs. I can talk with his voice. And I can think my own thoughts. But Gus is stronger than I am. His memories become my memories, too. This is new. I couldn't see into the past of the other bodies I've inhabited. I'm scared that Gus might reclaim his body and drown me in his blood.

And so here we are on the ridge above the Indian camp. The sun is hot over the hills. And Gus remembers—and I remember—what he saw when he came upon those slaughtered white settlers.

Dead white bodies stripped naked and mutilated and ruined.

There was the body of a little girl, blond, blue-eyed, pretty even in death. She was still wearing her little blue gingham dress. She was the only person still wearing her clothes. The Indians had shown her that much respect: They murdered her, but they didn't strip her naked. They let her die as an innocent.

Three arrows in her stomach. She was still clutching a rag doll.

Gus's eyes water at the memory. My eyes water.

I weep on the ridge above the Indian camp. I stare with watery vision down on the camp where that little girl's murderers are sleeping and eating and laughing and telling stories and having sex and dancing and singing.

It's Indians down there. And I'm an Indian. But we're not all the same kind of Indians, are we?

No, those Indians down there killed a little girl. Shot three arrows into her belly and left her to die. And two feet away from that little girl's body lay the naked body of a woman. Three arrows in her belly, too. A blond and blue-eyed woman, bloody and violated, her right hand forever reaching out toward the little girl.

Yes, the girl's mother, as she was dying, crawled across the grass toward her dying daughter and didn't make it.

The mother died two feet away from her daughter. Separated. They are cursed to be ghost mother and ghost daughter and will wander the grassy plains in the endless search for each other.

These are not my thoughts. This is not my sadness. This all belongs to Gus, and his grief and rage are huge, so my grief and rage are huge, too, and I scream as I lead one hundred soldiers down the hill into the Indian camp.

Eleven

This is what revenge can do to you.

I lead those one hundred soldiers down the hill toward the Indian camp.

We are killers.

As we ride to the bottom of the hill and race the short distance across the flats toward camp, I can feel Gus's rage and grief leaving my body. With each hoofbeat, I lose pieces of my rage, until I am left with only my fear.

I had wanted to kill, but now I just want to stop.

I throw away my rifle. I don't want to use it. But I keep riding. I am unarmed. I think I want to die. I think I want Gus to die.

I think I want to lose this fight.

We didn't really surprise the Indians with our attack. We didn't even try to sneak up on them. We
wanted them to know we were coming. And so, yes,
they knew we were coming, and they're ready.

But only twenty-five Indian warriors ride out to meet
us. Most of them are boys. And only a few of them have
rifles.

The rest have bows and arrows. And, sure, they're accurate. I see one soldier get hit in the chest with an
arrow and another get hit in the stomach.

But we have repeating rifles.

It's one hundred repeating rifles versus seven rifles and
eighteen bows.

We only lose a few men as we roar toward the Indian warriors. They are screaming and crying. They
must prevent us from reaching their camp. If we reach
it, we will kill old people, women, and children. We
will destroy families. But the warriors can't stop us.
They are riding to their deaths. And they are singing
their death songs.

Most of them fall before we're even close to them.
One hundred rifles equals one hundred bullets every
three seconds. In the twenty-one seconds it takes us to
close the distance, we shoot seven hundred bullets.

Only a few of the warriors survive that crash of bullets.

And then we swarm into them. Ninety-five surviving
white soldiers attack eleven Indian warriors. We barely

pause as we kill all of them, with bullet and fist and saber and boot.

I don't kill anybody. But I ride with killers, so that makes me a killer.

We ride into camp. There's only twenty or thirty tents arranged in loose circles. I don't know what tribe. Gus doesn't care. He almost makes me not care.

We are attacked as we ride through the camp. A few of the women have bows and arrows, too. And a few old men.

And one tiny Indian boy. He can't be more than five years old. He holds a bow. He is Bow Boy. Is he strong enough to even use his weapon? Can he pull back the string and let loose an arrow?

No, he can't.

He bloodies his fingers on the taut string. And he cries out in pain. But he keeps trying to shoot us. And he bloodies his hand again and again.

I see a soldier slam his horse into an old woman. She falls. The soldier spins his horse around and tramples her. He spins again and rides over her one more time.

A soldier dismounts and chases down a woman and her little daughter. He shoots the woman in the back. She falls. The daughter drops to her knees beside her mother. Daughter wails. The soldier shoots at the daughter. But his gun jams. He pulls the trigger again. Nothing. So he grabs the barrel of his rifle, still so hot that it burns his hands. But he doesn't feel the pain, not yet, as he smashes the gun down on the girl's skull. He hits her again and again. Keeps hitting her until his rifle breaks in half.

A group of soldiers, seven or eight of them, drag two screaming and kicking women into a tent.

A soldier jumps up and down on the belly and chest of an old man.

And everywhere, everywhere, other soldiers are shooting Indians.

Bullet after bullet after bullet after bullet.

I see General Mustache down on one knee, taking careful aim at the women and children and old people who flee from us. They run toward the faraway hills. To the thick woods on the faraway hills. Two or three miles away.

The general pulls the trigger. Again and again. And a person falls each time he shoots.

It's madness.

I wish I had kept my rifle so I could shoot myself. I don't want to see anymore. I want to be blind. I want to leave this place. I don't care where I go. I don't care about which body or time period is waiting for me. I will gladly float in the nowhere. I will gladly be a ghost, if I can be a ghost who can't see or hear.

And then a stray bullet strikes my horse. Blows my horse's head into pieces. Covers me with blood and launches me toward the sky.

I think the quickest prayer of my life as I fly: *Lord, please break my neck.*

And then I crash into the ground and roll through a campfire and land on a pile of dead bodies.

I scream.

I look up to see Bow Boy running. Oh, my God. He's only five years old. His hands are bloody. His father must have died with the other warriors. And his mother, oh, where is his mother?

And now I see a soldier running after Bow Boy. The soldier carries a saber—a sword—the simplest killing machine. This white soldier, a boy himself, maybe sixteen years old, chases Bow Boy.

Oh, Jesus, stop this. Oh, God, reach down and crush all of us like insects.

But when have Jesus and God ever stopped a man from taking revenge?

Bow Boy runs fast. The white soldier cannot catch him. Bow Boy spins in circles, dodges, ducks, and spins back toward me.

I stagger to my feet. I will protect him. I will save him.

I run toward Bow Boy, but I am old and hurt. My knees give out, and I stagger and fall again. I bloody my face in the dirt.

I look up to see Bow Boy fall, too. With saber raised high, the white soldier races toward Bow Boy. I am going to watch this murder.

This is my punishment. Yes, this is God's final punishment for me. I will watch this boy die.

But, no.

Wait.

Without stopping, that white soldier reaches down and picks up Bow Boy. Cradles the child in one arm. And the white soldier keeps running. He's running toward the faraway hills. Toward those faraway trees. Toward cover. Toward safety. Carrying an Indian child, a white soldier is running with Indians.

I can't believe it. It can't be true. But it is true.

That white soldier, a small saint, is trying to save Bow Boy.

I wonder if the other escaping Indians see this. I wonder if it gives them hope. I wonder if this act of love makes it easier for them to face death.

In the midst of all this madness and murder, one soldier has refused to participate. He has chosen the opposite of revenge. Somehow that one white boy, that small saint, has held on to a good and kind heart. A courageous and beautiful heart.

I have to help him.

The other soldiers haven't noticed Small Saint's escape. They are too busy with blood.

But they will see him soon enough. And they will kill him, too.

I stand and run–limp, looking for a rifle and a horse. My tools. I need my tools. The tools of war. The tools of revenge. The tools of offense and defense. Of attack and protection. Of good and evil.

I find a rifle, stringed with beads and buckskin, lying on the ground. One of the fallen warriors' guns, an ancient single-shot rifle. I don't even know if it works. But I pick it up and run after a painted pony that spins in circles. The pony doesn't know where to go.

I reach him, crawl painfully onto his back, and race after Small Saint and Bow Boy.

As I ride, I see that General Mustache has finally noticed them, too.

"It's a deserter!" Mustache yells. "He's gone Indian!"

What does that mean, *gone Indian*? I don't know. Mustache aims at Small Saint's back. Aiming for the center of mass. A kill shot. He will not miss.

I ride hard toward Mustache. He doesn't know I am coming. I don't know if I will reach him before he fires.

Small Saint runs with Bow Boy. Confused, terrified, Bow Boy struggles to get free. But Small Saint will not let go. He runs and runs and runs.

General Mustache takes careful aim. He wants to kill this traitorous soldier. He hates soldiers who refuse to kill. And he hates the ones who have killed but refuse to kill again. The ones who drop their weapons and run. The ones who drop their weapons and stand still. The ones who shoot themselves in the foot, heart, and head.

Traitors, all traitors.

I scream as I reach General Mustache. He turns and fires his weapon at me. But he misses wide as I swing my rifle and smash him in the face. He falls.

And I ride after Small Saint and Bow Boy.

Other soldiers pursue me. I can hear the curses and hoofbeats behind me. I can hear and feel their gunfire. All around me, running Indians, the old people, women, and children, so many of them fall to gunfire.

How many rifles are behind me? How many soldiers? I don't know.

Some part of me, the part that is Gus, wants me to stop, to turn around and re-swear my allegiance to the other soldiers. But I can defeat Gus now. I am doing the right thing. I am trying to save the soldier who is trying to save Bow Boy.

My painted pony is fast, faster than the other horses. He runs for his life, too. I wonder if the soldiers' horses are cursing this Indian pony. I wonder if horses judge each other based on their human riders.

I catch up to Small Saint and Bow Boy. For a second, Small Saint thinks he's been caught, that I am there to kill them.

But I reach out a hand, Small Saint grabs it, and I haul him and the boy on the horse, all of this at full gallop.

With his ancient broken body, Gus could never have done that. I own this body now.

And how can this small pony carry three people and not collapse or slow down?

Because of fear. Because of grace. Because we want to live.

Terrified, overloaded, on our powerful pony we outrace the soldiers and their horses.

We all race for the faraway hills. The faraway trees. Getting closer now, so close.

Faster, faster now, faster than I thought possible. I wonder if the pony will catch fire. If the pony has caught fire. If the pony is leaving behind hoofprints that spark and smolder.

We are two hundred yards from the trees, one hundred yards, fifty yards.

I don't want to look behind me, but the sounds of gunfire and hooves and curses grow fainter and fainter. We are leaving our enemies behind. They will not catch us on horseback. But they can still catch us with gunfire.

I hear the bullets sizzle past us.

Thirty, twenty, ten yards. The pony leaps into the air. It grows wings and flies into the forest.

No, of course not. It doesn't grow wings. How can a horse grow wings?

That kind of extraordinary magic is not permitted here. No, the only magic here is ordinary. It's so ordinary that it might not be magic at all. It might only be luck.

But I'll take luck.

As we crash through the underbrush and leap over stumps and fallen trees, I praise luck. As we leave behind the soldiers who want to kill us, who have killed so

many others, I praise luck. As I hear the weeping of
Small Saint and Bow Boy, who are happy to be alive,
however temporarily, I praise luck. As we outrun horses
and bullets, as we outrun that monster revenge, I praise
luck.

Twelve

This is what it feels like to be old.

After crashing headfirst off a horse into a campfire, and swinging two people onto the back of your pony with one arm, and all the excitement of outrunning killer soldiers with rifles, you have a few bruises and burns and scrapes and cuts and sore muscles.

In fact, after you ride fast and hard a mile or two into the trees, and think you have left behind your enemies, you need to slow down.

And when an old guy relaxes, when the fear juices leave his body, he is immediately reminded of exactly how old he is.

How old am I? How old is this body?

After I relax, my back seizes up. It goes completely stiff, like I'm made out of steel. And I fall off my pony.

I hit the ground and hurt my ribs. I think I might have cracked something. I can barely breathe.

Small Saint and Bow Boy are still on the horse. Small Saint has taken the reins and spins the pony back toward me.

There are sixteen tiny little men with sharp knives slashing my spine. I'm curled into a ball. And every time I try to straighten up, or even move or breathe, another tiny little guy shows up with a sharp knife.

If the soldiers caught up to us right now, I wouldn't be able to defend myself. They could walk right up to me and I'd just be curled into a ball like a bug. And one of them, or all of them, would raise their boots and squish me.

I'm useless.

And then it's over. My back relaxes. The knife-wielding little guys run away. And I can slowly straighten my back. I don't want to stand up yet. I can still feel little tremors in my muscles, as if my body was just waiting and preparing for another big quake. Or for those little bastards to come back with chain saws.

So I lie on the ground and I look up at Small Saint and Bow Boy still on the pony. The Indian boy has curled into the white soldier. Has his little arms wrapped around the soldier's neck. Bow Boy loves Small Saint like he was his father. Or his mother. Or both.

I remember I used to be like that little boy, holding tightly on to anybody who showed me even the tiniest bit of love. I haven't been like that in a long time.

"Are you okay, sir?" Small Saint asks me.

"Define okay," I say.

Small Saint smiles. He's missing half his teeth. I guess dental care wasn't a high priority in the nineteenth century.

"We can't stay here long, sir," Small Saint says. "They're going to be coming after us. They're not going to let us go."

He's right. I'm not a soldier, but I know that we just did about two million of the worst things any soldier can do. We disobeyed orders. I smacked a general in the face with a rifle. I might have killed him.

And I think I broke my rifle. I notice I'm still holding on to it. The rifle covered with buckskin and beads. It was an Indian warrior's rifle; now it's mine. I wonder if it works. Did I break it when I smashed it over the general's head?

And how much I already love this weapon. It saved me. It saved Small Saint and Bow Boy. I didn't have to fire a bullet to use it.

Even after falling off the pony, I kept hold of this rifle. An old soldier's reflexes, I guess. Or maybe it's because my hands are frozen shut from that arthritis stuff.

I'm not much of a hero.

Small Saint and I saved an Indian kid. That makes us traitors. And traitors are never, ever forgiven or forgotten.

"I just need to rest a few more minutes," I say. "My back is fucked. I'm afraid it will knock me down again if I try to stand up too soon."

I laugh at my accent. I'm trying to sound like me, but I can only sound like Irish Gus.

"I'm Irish," I say.

"My granddaddy's from there, sir," Small Saint says.

Bow Boy doesn't say anything.

"Are you about ready to get up, sir?" Small Saint says. He keeps looking back and listening hard. "They're out there coming. I can feel them."

"I think I might have broken a rib," I say. "It hurts to breathe."

"I know you're hurting, sir," Small Saint says. "I'm hurting. Indian boy's hurting. We're all hurting, sir, but we're going to be hurting a lot more if they catch us."

I know I should get up. I want to get up. But I can't seem to find the willpower.

All I know is that I need to stand, shake off the pain and fear, get back on that pony, and ride away from here.

And I'm going to get up in a minute.

I'm going to stand in a second.

Any moment now.

Right now.

Pretty soon.

Any moment.

"Sir," Small Saint says. "I hate to bother you again. But we really need to go now. Right now. I can hear them coming."

I listen hard. I can't hear anything. But I've got old ears. I'm tired and broken and beaten, and I don't know if I can get up. Part of me wants to become a part of the dirt and grass.

Other soldiers are coming to kill me, and I can't even find the courage or strength to stand up. I know that it would be easier to give up than to stand up. Easier for me.

But Bow Boy and Small Saint need me.

I need me.

So I roll over onto my stomach, onto my hands and knees, and push myself up. I'm on my feet. My back trembles. I can feel the little pain that wants to be bigger pain.

Come on, Gus! Toughen up!

I take a little step. I'm walking! I take a big step! I look around for my adoring audience. I feel like I need applause. I'm up and ready to go. I'm up and ready to run from the killers.

"All right, kid," I say to Small Saint. "Let's go."

"You want to ride with us?" he asks.

"No, I think it's better for my back if I walk."

So Small Saint and Bow Boy ride the pony and I walk. And we begin our slow-motion escape.

With my old ears, I can hear the soldiers catching up to us.

"How far back you think they are?" I ask Small Saint.

"Maybe three miles, sir. Probably closer to two."

"Can we outrun them?" I ask.

I know that Gus is supposed to be the experienced

scout, but I'm not going to make guesses. This kid knows more than I do.

He's thinking hard.

"Can we outrun them?" I ask again.

"Probably not, sir," he says. "But we have to try."

"How long before they catch us?"

"At this rate, ten–fifteen minutes, maybe."

"All right, then," I say, because I don't know what else to say. And then I think to ask something else. "Hey, kid," I say. "Why'd you do it?"

"Do what, sir?" Small Saint asks.

"Why'd you save the Indian boy?"

Small Saint thinks for a moment. "I joined the military to defend people," he said. "And that's what I'm doing right now."

I will never be as good or as brave as this kid.

I try to walk faster, and then I jog a bit. My knees and back are hurting. But I pick up the pace. I'm trying to replace Gus's old body with my young spirit.

I'm trying to replace Gus's knees with my knees.

And so Small Saint pushes the pony to a slow trot. And I'm pushing Gus to a slow trot. And we go.

I know I won't be able to keep up this pace. I know this chase is unfair. But we have to run. We have to keep running.

And so we run.

Behind us, the curses and hoofbeats of the cavalry. Ahead of us, who knows?

Behind us, death.

And so we run.

And then I trip over a fallen branch and fall beside it. My back seizes up again. I curl. And I scream.

"Sir!" Small Saint shouts. "Sir! Are you okay?"

All I can do is scream. The pain is so huge, like a thousand little men are digging a train tunnel through my back.

Please, please, make the pain stop.

"Sir!" Small Saint shouts. "Sir! What should I do?"

The soldiers are so close now, I imagine I can smell them. I smell gunpowder and sweat and blood and hate.

"Go!" I yell. "Run!"

"But what about you, sir!" Small Saint shouts. "I won't leave a man behind, sir!"

"You have to! Go! Go!"

"No, sir! No, sir!"

I can tell by the look in his eyes that he's ready to make his stand here. That he will fight a million soldiers to save the Indian boy.

But this is not supposed to be his end.

There are two children riding that pony. They're supposed to be children and stay children for as long as possible.

"You have to save him!" I shout. "Save the kid!"

And now Small Saint understands. He knows he might escape if he leaves me behind. He knows he has a better chance. It's a horrible choice to make, but he must make it.

"I'll hold them off," I say. "I'll buy you more time."

How crazy. I can't even uncurl my back and I'm going to fight charging cavalry soldiers?

"Go," I say. "Please."

It's the *please* that does it. Funny how a little politeness can change people's minds.

Small Saint salutes me and then he's off, galloping at full tilt, to disappear into the dark trees.

I'm lying alone.

The soldiers ride closer and closer.

In great pain, I roll over on my stomach, and then crawl to a log. My cover. I brace my rifle on the log. I don't even know if this old Indian rifle works anymore. But I'm going to try.

I take careful aim at the tree line.

The cavalry roars closer and closer, just minutes and seconds away.

I take careful aim. Then I laugh. This journey started when I shot a bunch of strangers in a bank. A horrible, evil act. And now I'm lying in the dirt, getting ready to shoot a bunch of other strangers. This time in self-defense and in defense of the two boys who are riding farther and farther away from me.

Is there really a difference between that killing and this killing? Does God approve of some killing and not other killing? If I kill these soldiers so that Small Saint and Bow Boy can escape, does that make me a hero?

I don't know. How am I supposed to know? I don't even have a good guess.

I take careful aim at the trees. In my fear, I realize the trees look like people. Giants. An audience of eager giants. All waiting for the show.

Me versus the soldiers.

I take careful aim at the dozen soldiers who crash into my view. They see me and curse and laugh. They are happy to have caught me. They ride hard toward me.

The general is with them. His face a mass of bloody bandages.

I take careful aim. I don't know if I have the heart to kill them. Isn't that odd? I once filled a room with bullets. I shot people who would never do me harm. And now I'm not sure I can shoot at the men who plan to kill me.

I hear screaming. I realize it is me screaming.

I hear weeping. I realize it is me weeping.

I close my eyes.

Thirteen

I'm flying.

I open my eyes in an airplane: a small plane. There's enough room for two or three people, but I'm alone.

I'm the pilot. I'm inside the body of the pilot.

No, I have become the pilot. I don't feel separate from him.

I fly just below a ceiling of clouds and above the ocean. If I flipped the plane over, the ocean would be my ceiling and the clouds my floor, and it would not matter.

It is my plane, the clouds, the ocean, and me. All of it is beautiful and interchangeable. All of it is equally important and unimportant. All of it is connected.

I am the pilot and the clouds and the ocean and the plane.

Man, this has to be Heaven.

I laugh.

Yes, it is Heaven.

I have survived my journey through time and place and person and war and have now arrived in my Heaven.

And my Heaven is a small airplane that will forever fly. It will never land.

Maybe that sounds boring. A small part of me thinks, *Well, yeah, that is boring.* But I am happy right now. It feels like the kind of happy that can last forever.

I wonder about Small Saint and Bow Boy. Did they escape? What happened after I left old Gus's body? Did he suddenly wake up and shit himself when he saw his old friend General Mustache shooting at him?

But I can't wonder and worry too much. I'll go insane, I think. But if being crazy means I get to fly a plane, then I'll take crazy.

The really funny thing is that I'm scared of flying. Terrified, really.

I've only been on two flights before: the one to visit New York with that rich Seattle do-gooder and the other with my mother. When she was pregnant with me. I know I'm not supposed to remember it. And I don't remember it, not really. But I can feel it. I have the memory of it in my DNA.

I have the photograph of my mother sitting in the airplane: a big jet. I don't know who took the photograph. I think it was my Indian father. I think so because my mother smiles in that photograph. She stares into the camera and smiles.

It's obvious that my mother loved my father.

A few months after that photograph, my mother was in labor with me, and my father was leaving. By the time my mother held me, a newborn, in her arms, my father was already hundreds of miles away, never to return.

Fucking bastard.

And then six years after he left, my mother was dead of breast cancer. I think she missed my father so much that it killed her. I think her sadness caused her cancer. I think her grief grew those tumors.

I miss my mother. I miss her all the time. I want to see her again. And now here I am in the body of a pilot as he flies.

It makes sense.

The last time my mother was happy she was on an airplane. So maybe this is my last place to be happy. Maybe I'll be as happy as my mother. Maybe I am flying to meet her.

But no, that's not it.

I can feel this body remembering. Every part of you has different memories. Your fingers remember the feel of a velvet coat. Your feet remember a warm sandy beach. Your eyes remember a face.

My eyes remember a face.

I remember a brown-skinned man. Black hair, curly black hair. Brown eyes. Eyeglasses. A short man, thin but muscular. He wore a black shirt and blue jeans every day of his life, every day that I knew him. Who is he? Who is this man I'm remembering? Is it me? Am I the man I am remembering?

No, I am a pale man. Blond, blue-eyed. Big. Strong. I fill up this airplane.

I am much larger than the man I am remembering. I am reconstructing him. His name is Abbad. He is an Ethiopian, a Muslim.

He's lived in the United States for fifteen years. Came here for college, to study mechanical engineering, and never went back home.

I look over at the empty seat beside me, and Abbad is there. Or the memory of him is there. Or his ghost is there.

"Jimmy," he says to me, "tell me the truth. You must tell me the truth."

His English is slightly accented. It is a beautiful accent. Abbad is a beautiful man. Small and dark and beautiful.

"You cannot hide the truth from me, Jimmy," Abbad says, and laughs. "I can smell your lies. They smell like onions and beer."

My name is Jimmy. I am Jimmy the pilot.

"Abbad," I say, "I didn't think you were a terrorist."

"You are a liar, Jimmy. When I came to your door, when I said, *I want to be a pilot,* you immediately thought of September eleventh. You immediately thought I was another crazy terrorist who wanted to learn how to fly planes into skyscrapers."

"No, I didn't."

"Yes, you did. Of course you did. And do you know how I know you thought such things?"

"How?"

"Because I was turned away from seven flight instructors before I came to you. One flight instructor pulled a gun on me."

"Now *you're* lying," I say.

"I wish I were lying," Abbad says. "But no, he told me to wait a minute while he grabbed some paperwork. Then he went into the back room and came out with a shotgun. He called me a sand nigger and said he was going to blow off my head if I didn't get the fuck out of his place of business."

Abbad laughs.

"You Americans love capitalism so much," he says. "That man didn't tell me to get out of his house, or out of his life. He didn't tell me to go to hell or back to Africa or back to wherever he thought I came from. No, he told me to get out of his *place of business*. Business! That's all he could think about."

Abbad laughs.

What kind of man can laugh at such a horrible story? A kind and funny and forgiving man.

"So, Jimmy, now tell me the truth. You thought I was a terrorist, didn't you?"

I laugh.

"You did, didn't you?" Abbad asks.

"Yes," I say. "Maybe I was a little worried about you."

"Ha, see, I knew it," Abbad says, and laughs. He rocks back and forth in his seat. The small plane bounces. Abbad is happy turbulence.

"And now? What do you think now?" Abbad asks.

"I think you're an asshole," I say.

Abbad laughs even louder. He laughs so hard that he chokes. Coughing and choking, he keeps laughing. I laugh with him.

We are friends.

And then Abbad is gone. His memory fades away. And I am alone in the airplane again.

I can fall so far inside a person, inside his memories, that I can play them like a movie.

And I can feel the pilot's emotions. He misses Abbad. Misses him very much. I can feel his heartbreak.

Jimmy's hands work the controls, switching buttons, flipping switches, guiding the plane from left to right across the sky. I guess that pilots call it port and starboard, but I call it left and right. It's all I know. But it doesn't matter that I'm a flying moron. I have nothing to do with this. I am a spectator.

And that's okay. I can relax and enjoy the flight.

This is not Heaven, after all, but it feels great to fly. Jimmy is not afraid of flying, so I'm not afraid. I have borrowed his courage and joy, as well as his sadness and regret.

And I feel the joy and sadness in equal parts as Jimmy floats the plane lower and lower toward a small airport.

I see the airport in the distance. Landing lights, control tower, terminal, hangar. All is gold and green.

Jimmy smiles as the plane touches down. I understand that he never takes flight for granted. He is always happy to fly and happier to land safely.

He taxies the plane into the hangar and shuts it down.

He opens the door, steps out onto the wing, and jumps down onto the floor. He walks over to a large sink, fills a bucket with soap and water, and begins to wash his airplane.

He does this with great care, even affection.

As he washes each airplane part, he says its name aloud: *stabilizer, rudder, lift, wing, elevator, aileron, spoiler, slat, wheel*.

I remember my mother naming my parts as she bathed me. How could I remember that? I was just a baby. She had to wash me in a tub that sat on the kitchen table. Do I really remember that? Or am I pretending to remember it?

As Jimmy washes his plane, he again remembers Abbad. And as he remembers, Abbad appears again. Also carrying a bucket and sponge.

"Jimmy, you are a fool," Abbad says. "You have a beautiful wife at home and you spend all your time with your airplane."

"My airplane is more dependable," Jimmy says.

"Ah, you Americans, you let your wives control your destiny. That is not our way."

"You're full of it, Abbad. You might think you control your women, but it's always the other way around. Muslim women just have to be craftier. They can't say they're in charge, but they're in charge."

"No. My wife knows that I wear the big pants in our family."

"You mean you wear the pants."

"That's what I said."

"No, you said big pants. They're just pants."

"I don't understand."

Abbad's English is nearly perfect, better than most native speakers, but he doesn't know how to use clichés.

Abbad shakes his head. "That doesn't make sense," he says. "How can you be the king if you don't have big pants?"

"Forget it," Jimmy says.

"I don't forget anything," Abbad says. And he says it so seriously that it makes Jimmy laugh.

It makes me laugh.

And then Abbad's cell phone rings. He looks at the caller ID.

"It's my wife," he says.

"Aren't you going to talk to her?"

"No, she's still mad at me because I forgot to bring home milk last night."

Abbad stares at the caller ID for a moment, then he smiles. And laughs.

Jimmy laughs, too.

"I guess I am the king of milk," Abbad says.

The men laugh harder. The laughter echoes in the hangar. And then it fades away.

Abbad fades away.

Jimmy is alone again with his airplane.

No, he's not alone.

"Hello, Jimmy." A woman's voice.

She's standing in a nearby doorway. She wears a T-shirt and blue jeans. She's young, maybe twenty. Red hair, green eyes. And she's pretty. Very short and very curvy. Cheerleader curvy.

I hope this is Jimmy's wife. And I wonder why he wants to spend more time with his airplane than he does with this woman.

"Hello, Helda," he says.

Helda! Her name is Helda? How does a beautiful girl get such an ugly name? Her parents must have been cruel and cold people.

"How was it up there today?" she asks.

"Beautiful. I could see for miles and miles," he says. "You should let me take you up."

"No way," she says. "You know I hate flying."

"You'll get over it," Jimmy says. I can feel his impatience with her. He wants her to love flying as much as he does.

"Are you hungry?" Helda asks.

I can't believe her name is Helda.

"I could eat," he says.

"Good, I brought a little picnic."

Jimmy walks into the office. She's laid out a feast on a blanket on the floor. Bread, fruit, fried chicken, wine. Wow, this woman is romantic. She's trying to woo Jimmy. Oh, that's so cute. Their marriage must be fragile. Married people only have picnics when their marriages are in trouble. I read that somewhere. But Jimmy is touched by this. I can feel his happiness. It makes me happy.

"Have a seat," she says.

Jimmy sits on the floor. He grabs a piece of fried chicken, a leg, and takes a bite. It's a little dry. So, okay, Helda isn't much of a cook. But that's okay. That's perfectly okay. Because she turns on a CD player and starts dancing.

She dances for Jimmy! Dances for me!

This has never happened to me before. And from the way that Jimmy feels, I don't think it's happened to him before either.

And that's sad. You'd think some beautiful woman would have danced for Jimmy before today.

But who's to judge? Helda dances for Jimmy now. She sexes their marriage. And I'm getting to enjoy a little bit of that sex.

I wonder if Helda will take off her clothes.

And then I hear another woman's voice. Or, rather, I hear a choked sob.

I turn to see another woman standing in the doorway. She's older, gray-haired, a little bit pretty and a little bit chubby. Her brown eyes are huge. Her knees buckle. But she catches her balance, puts a hand against the doorjamb for support, and covers her mouth. She sobs.

Then she turns and runs away.

"Who was that?" Helda asks.

"My wife," Jimmy says.

Fourteen

Okay, so I guess that Jimmy the pilot is a dirty liar and a cheat.

My Indian father was a dirty liar and a cheat.

So I guess this is another kind of justice. I've been dropped into the body of a man just like my father.

But I do know that Jimmy feels terrible. There's acid bubbling in his stomach and rising up his throat into his mouth. It tastes awful. Burning awful. I guess that's what guilt tastes like.

"Jesus," Helda says. "I didn't mean—"

She doesn't know what to say. She just stands there and stares at the doorway where Jimmy's wife used to be.

"She's never been here before," Jimmy says. "I've been flying planes for twelve years, and never, not once in all that time, has she ever come down here."

Jimmy is a traitor. I'm mad at him, sure, but I also feel sorry for him. Or maybe he's just feeling sorry for himself, and so I feel him feeling sorry.

"What are we going to do?" Helda asks.

Jimmy looks at her. He doesn't love her. I can feel that he doesn't love her.

He is having an affair with a woman he doesn't love. So he's cheating on her, too, sort of. I mean, I don't think you're supposed to have sex with people you don't love. I know, I know, I know. People do it all the time. But I really think you're supposed to be a little bit in love with them. At least a tiny bit. And I can feel that Jimmy doesn't love Helda at all. In fact, he thinks she's irritating.

"Jimmy," Helda says again. "What are we going to do now?"

"I'm going to go find my wife," Jimmy says.

"But what about me?" she asks.

"I love my wife," Jimmy says.

Helda starts crying.

Jimmy is a major-league jerk. He's made two women weep and wail in two minutes. And he made Helda cry by saying, "I love my wife." I mean, normally, those four words are romantic and lovely, right? But right now they're as cold and sharp as an icicle stabbed into the heart.

Why do people hurt each other like this?

I just know I never want to be as much in love with anybody as these women are in love with Jimmy. You can't trust people with your love. People will use your love. They'll take advantage of you. They'll lie to you. They'll cheat you.

"I love my wife," Jimmy says again.

"But what about me?" Helda asks.

"I have to go," Jimmy says.

He leaves her like that. I try to make him stay. I try to hold him back. But I have zero control of his body. I try to influence his mind. I shout. But he can't hear me.

He walks out the door and leaves Helda behind. I can hear her crying hard as Jimmy walks into the parking lot. Jimmy jumps into a big pickup and drives off.

He thinks about betrayal, so I think about betrayal.

He thinks of how many wives and husbands are cheating on each other. And thinks of how many fathers are abandoning their children. He thinks of how many people are going to war against other people. We're all betraying one another all the time.

I think how I betrayed those people in the bank. Those people in the bank trusted me to be sober and smart and kind. I betrayed them. I'm a betrayer.

I want to weep, but it's kind of hard to do that when you don't have a body. I want to make Jimmy weep for me, but his eyes are filled with his own tears.

He's crying about his marriage and he's crying about other shit, too.

He's crying about Abbad, I think, because that beautiful brown man suddenly materializes in the truck with us.

"Jimmy, Jimmy," he says, "you Americans are so arrogant. You think the whole world wants to be like you."

"All I know for sure is this," Jimmy says. "You've lived in our country for fifteen years. And you've done really well—for yourself, for your wife, and for that new baby. Fifteen years, Abbad, fifteen good years."

"Yes, Jimmy," Abbad says. "I've lived here for fifteen years, and I have been sad and lonely for my real home on every one of my days. I live in the United States because my real home has been destroyed."

Abbad is crying. He wipes his eyes and fades away.

Jimmy is alone in his truck. He drives fast.

He has destroyed his home, his marriage. He drives fast.

He has turned his wife into a refugee.

Jimmy drives into a small town, turns a corner onto a quiet street, and pulls into the driveway of a green house: his home.

His wife is there, too. And she's throwing his clothes out the front door onto the lawn: shirts, pants, shoes.

Jimmy sits in the truck and watches.

She's now throwing out magazines and books and CDs and DVDs and trophies and everything else that might belong to him.

Jimmy sits and watches.

Then she throws out plastic airplanes, toy airplanes, model airplanes, remote control airplanes. They crash onto the lawn. They crash into the apple tree in the front yard. They crash onto the driveway. They glide and crash into the street.

Five, ten, fifteen, twenty little plane crashes.

Jimmy sits and watches it happen. He watches his wife destroy all his things.

He knows he deserves it.

She carries out photo albums, opens them up, and tears out any photo of Jimmy, any photo that includes Jimmy, and any photo that reminds her of Jimmy.

Soon enough she realizes that every photo reminds her of Jimmy, so she throws all the photo albums into the yard.

She wants to tear out the parts of her brain and heart that remember Jimmy, but she can't do that. So she tears off her wedding ring and throws that into the street. It clinks against the pavement and rolls and rolls and rolls and disappears.

That takes the last of her energy. She falls to her knees on the porch. She pushes her forehead against the floor and she weeps.

Jimmy sits and watches.

I wonder if my mother mourned like this when my father left her. I wonder if Jimmy's wife will get cancer from her sadness.

Finally, Jimmy gets out of his truck and walks toward his wife. He steps over and around his things strewn all over the lawn. He steps onto the porch and stands above his wife.

"Linda," he says.

Her name is Linda. A simple, pretty name.

"Linda," he says again.

She doesn't respond. She keeps weeping.

"Linda," he says, for the third time.

Without looking up, without moving, she speaks.

"How long has this been going on, Jimmy?"

"A year, thirteen months," he says.

"Do you love her?"

"No."

She wails louder. Why is she crying harder now? I don't understand. Would it have been better if he'd said yes?

"Linda," he says, for the fourth time.

Does this guy think he can fix things if he keeps saying her name? Is he that stupid? He might be. People are that stupid.

"Did you ever do it in our bed?" she asks.

"No," he says.

"You're lying," she says. "Tell me the truth, okay? For once, tell me the truth. Did you sleep with her in our bed?"

"Yes," he says.

Linda suddenly sits up. She pulls a pistol from her coat, a little pistol, and points it at Jimmy.

And at me.

Fifteen

Jimmy wants to die.

As he stands there and stares at the pistol in his wife's hand, Jimmy realizes he wants her to pull the trigger.

Jimmy wants his wife to kill him.

That's crazy.

But it happens all the time, right?

Strangers hardly ever kill strangers. All over the world, thousands of times a day, husbands and wives kill one another.

It's mostly husbands killing wives, I think.

But sometimes a wife will kill a husband.

Like, right now, as Linda points a pistol at Jimmy and pulls the trigger.

Click.

Jimmy doesn't flinch. Doesn't move.

"I took the bullets out," Linda says. "I just wanted to see you shit your pants, you bastard."

But Jimmy is strangely disappointed. He wants to be punished for his crimes. I want to be punished for my crimes.

"Why are you just standing there?" Linda asks. "Aren't you going to say anything to me?"

"I wish there were bullets in the gun," Jimmy says.

"You're sad," she says. "You've always been so sad."

I can feel his sadness. It feels like he's wearing a sad coat with rocks in his pockets.

"I'm going to my mother's," Linda says. "And when I come back, I want you and your shit gone. I don't ever want to see you again."

"Okay," Jimmy says.

"Is that all you have to say?" she asks. "*Okay*? That's all you're going to say? Married for twenty years and all you've got for me is *okay*?"

"Yeah," Jimmy says.

"Fuck you, Jimmy." She walks over to her little car and drives away.

Jimmy looks around his yard. A few neighbors are watching. They've heard the fight. They're not surprised. They expected this to happen someday.

Jimmy thinks he should clean up the yard. He thinks he should throw everything into the back of his truck and drive away. And he does start the cleanup. He picks up a broken model plane, a DC-10. It's snapped in half.

He carries the broken plane into the house and sits in his chair in the living room.

He sits there alone and quiet for a long time.

He stares at the blank television.

And then a memory comes to him. And me.

That memory plays on the television.

It's a home video of Abbad. He's speaking directly to the camera. And then he's shouting in a foreign language, his language. I don't know what he's saying, but he's angry. Furious.

Then another home video, shot from a boat in the harbor, of a passenger airplane falling from the sky into downtown Chicago. An explosion. Flames rising.

Then a photograph of Abbad, his wife, and his baby.

Then a news reporter speaks.

"Late this afternoon, in Chicago's Midway Airport, Abbad X and his wife and baby daughter boarded a commuter flight along with thirty-six other passengers. Shortly after takeoff, it appears that Abbad took over the airplane. The details are not clear at this time, but it appears that Abbad and his wife somehow disabled the passengers and crew. Abbad then took control of the airplane and crashed it into downtown Chicago during rush hour."

More video of cars and buildings on fire. Fire trucks, ambulances, police cars.

"All passengers on the airplane died instantly, and it appears that dozens of people on the ground have been injured. Police won't speculate on the number, but initial

estimates are that at least nine people on the street have
been killed."

A video of a little boy, weeping and wailing, as a fireman carries him through the smoke.

Jimmy taught Abbad how to fly a plane. And once
you know how to fly a plane, you also know how to
crash it.

Jimmy sits in his chair and stares at the blank television.

*Oh, Abbad, you are a murderer. Oh, Abbad, you are a
betrayer.*

Furious, Jimmy stands and throws the pieces of his
model plane across the room. They crash into a wall and
break into more pieces.

How can Jimmy ever be aerodynamic again?

He runs out to his truck, jumps in, and speeds away.

He remembers the reporters who came to his door.
The first one, a woman, promised to be fair.

"Jimmy," she said. "What can you tell us about Abbad?"

Jimmy could not answer the question. He didn't want
to answer the question.

"Jimmy," she said. "You taught Abbad how to fly a
plane. How did it make you feel when he used that
knowledge to kill dozens of people?"

He could not answer that question. He didn't want
to asnwer it.

"Jimmy," she said. "Do you want to defend yourself?"

He could not defend himself. He didn't want to defend himself. He was guilty. He had not murdered any-

body. He had never wanted to hurt anybody. But it was his fault. He had trusted Abbad.

Jimmy races his truck back to the airport. He pulls into the parking lot, jumps out, and runs into the hangar.

Helda is gone. Linda is gone. Abbad is gone. Everybody is gone, gone, gone.

Jimmy climbs into his airplane, starts it up, and taxis onto the runway.

He takes off, lifting his plane into the sky.

The clouds are the ceiling, the ground is the floor. Everything is green and golden.

Flight is supposed to be beautiful. It's supposed to be pure.

"Okay, Abbad, are you ready to take the controls?" Jimmy says.

Abbad materializes in the next seat.

"I don't know if I'm ready," Abbad says. "I don't think I'm ready to do it alone."

"You're not alone," Jimmy says. "I'm right here."

"Okay, okay, just give me a moment. I'll be ready in a moment. Just give me a moment."

"I'm right here, Abbad. Just trust me, okay? Just trust the plane. She'll take care of you."

Abbad reaches out and takes the controls. The plane feels lighter than it should.

"Okay, you have the helm," Jimmy says. "You have control."

Abbad flies the plane. He's smiling. And then he laughs.

"I'm flying!" Abbad screams.

"Yes, you are," Jimmy says. "How does it feel?"

"It's beautiful, it's so beautiful. Nothing is as beautiful as this."

Jimmy laughs at Abbad's poetry. He has heard it before. All first-time pilots have this moment, when they see the face of God in the sky ahead of them.

"Ah, fuck the birds!" Abbad shouts. "Fuck them, they get to fly like this whenever they want!"

Yes, Jimmy thinks. Yes, fuck the birds and their fucking wings.

Jimmy remembers Abbad's first landing, how they skidded to a sideways stop.

"Jimmy, I almost wrecked your plane," Abbad said.

"It's okay, first landings are always rough," Jimmy said.

"What would you have done if I wrecked your plane?"

"I would have killed you."

They laughed.

Jimmy remembers getting drunk with the less than devout Abbad later that night. In celebration.

"To Abbad!" Jimmy toasted.

"To flight!" Abbad toasted.

They drank whiskey and wine and good beer and cheap beer. They talked about sex and love and marriage and planes and religion and politics and both kinds of football.

Too drunk to drive, they walked back to the airport and fell down on the hangar floor beneath Jimmy's glorious airplane.

"To your plane!" Abbad toasted.

"Her name is Linda!" Jimmy shouted. His plane and his wife. Jimmy's two loves shared the same name.

"To Linda!" Abbad toasted.

"To Linda!" Jimmy agreed.

Lying on the floor, Jimmy reached out and grabbed Abbad's hand.

"You are my best friend," Jimmy said.

"You are my brother," Abbad said.

Oh, Abbad, you are a murderer. Oh, Abbad, you are a betrayer.

Alone in his airplane, Jimmy flies. I am with him. Jimmy flies out over the water, over the great lake, until the blue of the water and the blue of the sky are the same blue. He flies until he cannot see any land. Then he pushes down on the controls and sends the plane plummeting toward the water.

As we fall, I think about my mother and father. I think about the people I loved. I think about the people I hated. I think about the people I betrayed. I think about the people who have betrayed me.

We're all the same people. And we are all falling.

I close my eyes and pray.

Jimmy stays silent all the way down.

Sixteen

When I open my eyes I am staring at a rat.

No, wait.

The rat stares at me.

It's a huge wharf rat, two feet long, with intelligent eyes. And the rat seems to be thinking, *You're too big to kill, but I'm going to take a bite out of your ass anyway.*

I panic and roll away, thinking that the rat's violent intentions might actually be amorous. What if I've dropped into the body of a rat? What if I'm about to get fucked by another rat?

Shit.

But, no, I feel human. I am human. A human who rolls away from a rat.

I roll through rotten food and dog shit and rank water and moldy newspaper. And then I slam into a Dumpster. Damn, it hurts.

But I have no time to complain. What if that rat has followed me? What if it's ready to attack? I look back for it, my enemy.

It hasn't moved. It stares at me.

"Fuck you, rat," I say.

My words are quickly followed by projectile vomit. I spew half-digested food and booze toward the rat.

That scares it away, and I laugh.

Damn rat wasn't expecting that. Of course, if I hadn't scared him, the rat would have gladly eaten my vomit. And that disgusting thought makes me vomit again.

I retch. My stomach convulses. And I see blood in my vomit.

Am I dying?

Well, I'm certainly a street drunk, a loser whose belly is torn apart by booze. That's why they call it rotgut.

A cliché now, but somebody coined that word centuries ago. And imagine how funny and sad and accurate it was the first time somebody said it.

Yeah, that whiskey will rot your guts. It's rotgut.

Why the hell am I thinking this stupid shit? Probably because I'm still drunk.

"Hey, buddy!"

Somebody yells at me.

"Hey, buddy!"

I see two pairs of shoes walking toward me. I know those shoes are connected to legs, bodies, and faces, but I can't lift my head high enough to see any details.

"You all right, dude?" A young man's voice.

I roll onto my back and look up at a young man and woman. A couple. Pretty white people. Cameras around their necks, genuine concern in their eyes.

Gorgeous tourists.

"You okay?" the young man asks again.

"I'm drunk," I say.

"Yes, you are."

"What do I look like?" I ask.

"What do you mean?"

"Am I young or old?"

The young couple look at each other and laugh. I don't mean to amuse them. I just want to know whose body I've dropped into this time.

"Am I young or old?" I ask again.

"You look about fifty," the young woman says. "Like my father."

"Am I white?"

"No," she says. "You're Indian."

"How do you know I'm Indian?"

"Your braids. And your shirt."

I look down at my dirty T-shirt, emblazoned with a black-and-white photograph of the Apache warrior Geronimo and the ironed-on caption FIGHTING TERRORISM SINCE 1492.

"Do you need some help?" the young woman asks.

"What's your name?" I ask.

"Pam," she says. "And this is Paul."

"Pam and Paul," I say. "That's too fucking cute."

They laugh again. He laughs so hard that he stumbles and almost steps in my vomit. He dances and spins away from it, and that makes them laugh harder. Are they drunk, too?

"Where am I?" I ask. "What city?"

"Tacoma," Paul says.

Just thirty miles from Seattle. I'm getting closer to home, if not closer to my own body.

"What year is it?" I ask.

That makes them laugh, too.

"Dude," Paul says, "you are way drunk."

"Just tell me what year it is," I say. "Please."

"Two thousand seven," he says.

"It's now," I say.

"Well, no matter where you are, dude, it's always now, ain't it?"

Great, a fucking philosopher.

"Can you help me get up?" I ask.

"Sure," he says.

Pam and Paul help me to my feet. I'm dizzy. And I vomit again. Pam and Paul leap away as I fall to my knees. I vomit again.

And it's filled with blood, too much blood.

I must be dying.

"Dude," Paul says. "You need a doctor."

"Call nine-one-one," Pam says.

Paul pulls his cell phone out of his pocket and calls for help.

"They're on the way," he says.

But I don't want help.

No, wait. *This body* doesn't want help. I'm vomiting blood but I want to flee.

That doesn't make any sense. But I can't control my emotions. My fears. Yes, I'm afraid.

"I have to go," I say to Pam and Paul.

I don't want to say it. But I can't stop myself. This body is stronger than me. And this body wants to escape.

And so I run. No, I shamble.

Jesus, that's the absolute worst way in which any human can travel: shambling. Shit.

"Come back," Pam and Paul call after me. I can hear the concern in their voices, but I don't hear any passion. They're not going to detain me or follow me or let me become anything other than an anecdote to tell at dinner parties.

And then there was the time we helped this homeless Indian guy. . . .

Of course, they'd revise history in order to make themselves look more heroic, to give the story a happy fucking ending.

And then the ambulance came and saved him. And the paramedic said the Indian dude would have died if we'd called, like, five minutes later.

I don't look back at Pam and Paul as I continue to shamble away. I hate their alliteration almost as much as I hate their reflexive compassion.

I want to hurt them.

So I turn around and point a finger at them. I want to accuse them. To curse them.

"It's all your fault," I say.

"What?" Paul asks.

"It's all your fault," I say again.

"What's our fault?"

"White people did this to Indians. You make us like this."

I don't even know if I believe that. But I think this homeless body believes it. I think this fifty-year-old guy wants to blame somebody for his pain and his hunger.

But what if it's his fault? What if he made all the decisions that led him to this sad-ass fate?

Fuck me, I think, and fuck this body I'm occupying.

"And fuck you," I say to Pam and Paul. "And fuck your whiteness."

Jesus, I wonder if this homeless guy understands the difference between white and whiteness. And then I wonder if I should be so condescending, considering that I am this homeless guy.

"Please," Pam says. "We're just trying to help."

"Fuck you," I say again. I don't want to say it. Not really. But this homeless guy's anger is even stronger than my anger. And anger is never added to anger. It multiplies.

"The ambulance will be here soon," Pam says. "Please wait."

"Did you tell them I was Indian?"

"Yes," Paul says.

"Did you tell them I was homeless?"

"Yes."

"Then they ain't coming. Not for a long time, at least. I'm way down on their priority list."

"But you're important to us," Pam says.

I laugh.

But I can tell she means it. And I hate her for meaning it. Her sincerity makes her weak and easily manipulated.

"You want to fuck me?" I ask.

"What?" Pam and Paul say together.

"Do you want to fuck me?" I ask again, slowly.

I can see the sudden anger in Paul. His eyes go lightning. His hands make beautiful fists. Good. He's not a pussy. Great. I want him to hit me. I want to fight.

"Come on, Pam," he says. "Let's get out of here."

"She doesn't want to go with you," I say. "She wants to stay here and fuck me."

Paul takes a quick step toward me, but Pam grabs his arm.

"No," she says. "Leave him alone. He doesn't know what he's saying."

God, she's tough. She won't let me take away her compassion. Maybe she can't be manipulated. Maybe I can't defeat her with my rage and self-hatred.

Jesus, I don't understand her.

"He can't talk to you like that," Paul says.

"It's all he knows how to do," she says. "Don't let it get to you."

He relaxes a bit. I can tell that he listens to her. He pays attention. He takes her advice. He seeks her counsel. He respects her.

I hate him for it. And I hate her for inspiring him.

"Hey, Paul," I say. "Does she like it in the ass?"

She can't stop him this time. He rushes toward me and punches me in the face.

Seventeen

I think he broke my jaw.

I shamble through an alley, blood filling my mouth and nose, and wonder if a man can drown in his own blood. Well, yes, of course, a man can drown in his blood. But can he drown while walking? If I stay upright, will I stay alive?

This alley smells like rotten food. Huge Dumpsters and garbage cans line both sides. They're filled with expired food and half-eaten meals. This must be an alley between rows of restaurants.

Other homeless folks forage. Flocks of sparrows, pigeons, and seagulls forage. And murders of crows bully the other birds and bully the humans, too.

I wish I'd wake up inside a crow.

Nobody looks at me as I stagger past. I'm not an uncommon sight. I'm a beaten bloody Indian. Who turns to look at such a man? There are other beaten bloody Indians in this alley.

What do you call a group of beaten bloody Indians, a murder of Indians? A herd of Indians? A bottle of Indians?

I want the other Indians to recognize me. To shout out my name. But they are hungry. And their pain is more important than my pain.

I don't remember how I got here. I remember that Paul punched me. And then I remember stepping into this alley. I don't remember the in-between. I have lost time.

Losing time: That's all I know how to do now.

Jesus, I'm pathetic. Didn't I just force that poor guy to hit me? Didn't I want his violence? Fuck me. I'm leaving this alley.

I'm going to walk out of this sad-sack alley and find a bathroom. And I'm going to wash my face and clothes. No, I'll steal some clothes. Good clothes. A white shirt and black pants. And I'll steal good shoes, too. Black leather shoes, cap toes, with intricate designs cut into the leather. In good clothes, I can be a good man.

And so I shamble out of the alley. No, I suck in my stomach muscles, straighten my spine, and hold my head level and I strut out of the alley.

And I horrify my audience. People sprint around me. A few just turn around and walk in the opposite direction. One woman screams.

Jesus, I must look like a horror movie. But that doesn't matter. I am covered with the same blood that is inside everybody else. They can't judge me because of this blood.

"I want some respect," I say.

Nobody hears me. Worse, nobody understands me.

"I want some respect," I say again, louder this time.

A man walks around the corner, almost bumps into me, and then continues on. He didn't notice me. He didn't see my blood. I follow him. A gray man, he wears a cheap three-button suit with better shoes. He talks loudly into a Bluetooth earpiece.

"I want some respect," I say to him.

He stops, turns around, and looks at me. He regards me.

"I want some respect," I say.

"I'll call you back, Jim, I got some drunk guy talking to me," he says into his earpiece, and hits the hang-up button. And then he asks me, "What the fuck do you want, chief?"

He thinks the curse word will scare me. He thinks the curse word will let me know that he once shot a man just to watch him die.

"I knew Johnny Cash," I say, "and you ain't Johnny Cash."

The man laughs. He thinks I'm crazy. I laugh. I am crazy. He offers me a handful of spare change.

"There you go, chief," he says.

"I don't want your money," I say. "I want your respect."

The man laughs again. Is laughter all I can expect?

"Don't laugh at me," I say.

"All right, all right, chief," he says. "I won't laugh at you. You have a good day."

He turns to walk away, but I grab his shoulder. He grabs my wrist and judos me into the brick wall.

"All right, all right, chief," he says. "I don't want you touching me."

He could snap my bones if he wanted to. He could drive his thumb into my temple and kill me. I can feel his strength, his skill, his muscle memory.

It's my turn to laugh.

"What's so funny?" he asks.

"I'm just wondering how many white guys are going to beat my ass today."

"Chief, you keep acting this way and we're all going to beat your ass today."

We both think that's funny, so we laugh together. And we almost bond because of our shared amusement.

"I'm going to let you go," he says. "And when I do, I want us both to act like gentlemen, okay?"

"I want some respect," I say.

"Are you going to be a gentleman?"

"I want some respect."

"How many times are you going to say that?"

"I'm going to say it until I get some respect."

The man looks around. He realizes that he's pinned a bloody homeless man against a brick wall. Not one of his prouder moments. But he's scared to let me go.

"All right, all right," he says. "How do I show you some respect?"

Shit, I don't have an answer for that. And then I realize that respect isn't exactly what I want. This body wants respect. I don't know what I want. And I don't know how to define respect, for me or for this homeless guy. So I take a guess.

"Tell me a story," I say.

"You want me to tell you a story?"

"Yeah."

"And that will give you respect?"

"Yeah."

The guy pauses again. He is flabbergasted to be in this situation. And I'm flabbergasted that I have used the word *flabbergasted*. This homeless Indian has an old-fashioned vocabulary wired into his brain.

"All right," he says. "What kind of story do you want to hear?"

"Something personal," I say. "Something you haven't told anybody. Something secret."

"I can't tell you secrets," he says. "I don't even know you."

And then the guy realizes that he can tell me anything precisely *because* he doesn't know me. He realizes that any stranger can be your priest.

"All right," he says. "I got a bird story."

"Bird stories are my favorite stories."

"You liar," he says, and lets me go.

He takes a step back. I turn and face him. He waits to see if I'm going to attack him.

"I'm listening," I say.

"All right," he says. "I have a daughter, Jill. She's seven. And she's been crying about getting a pet. A dog, a cat, a turtle, anything with four legs, right?"

"Kids like pets," I say.

"Just let me tell the story, Captain Obvious," he says.

"Then tell it."

"So, okay, we don't want to get a cat or dog or turtle or whatever because we don't want to clean up shit. Or we don't want to clean up a lot of shit. So my wife and I, we go to the pet store, and we ask the clerk what kind of animal shits the least."

"Fish," I say.

"See there, that's what I thought, too. Little fish, little poop. But then the clerk says that fish might shit small but they shit in their own water—"

"—so the aquarium itself becomes one big shit," I say.

"Gallons of shit and piss," he says. "So the clerk says that snakes only eat once a month, so they only shit once a month."

"And then you asked him what kind of asshole father would give a snake to his seven-year-old daugher."

"Well, I didn't say it in so many words, but that's essentially what I said."

"Then what did the clerk say?"

"Bird."

"What?"

"He said parakeet."

"Small bird, small shit."

"Exactly."

"And you believed him?"

"Yeah, stupid of me, right? I mean, we took that little bird home and he was a shit-master. Poop, poop, poop everywhere."

"And you hated it, right?"

"Well, I didn't like the shit, but I loved that bird."

The man is embarrassed to admit that. I like him for it.

"You see, he was a smart little fucker," the man says. "Could talk, liked to dance to AC/DC, and sat on my shoulder."

"You let him out of his cage?" I ask.

"Well, his wings were clipped."

"A clipped-wing bird ain't a bird," I say.

"All right, all right, Dr. Earth First, I'm not the one who clipped them. He was clipped when we bought him. And it wasn't like we bought him to be a tiny little Thanksgiving dinner. We loved that bird. I loved him. My daughter named him Harry Potter."

"That's cute."

"Damn right, it's cute. You want to hear the cutest part?"

"Yeah."

"I'm the cook of the family, the domestic, and Harry Potter loved to sit on my shoulder while I was cooking and insult my food."

"No."

"Yes, my wife and daughter told him to say *Too much salt* and *I'm being poisoned* and *I want pizza instead.*"

"That's hilarious."

"Yes, it is. And there's more. You see, my daughter's favorite dish is pasta-anything. So I'm always boiling water. And Harry Potter is always sitting on my shoulder."

"Oh, shit," I say, already guessing at the end of the story.

"You got that right. A few days ago, Harry Potter jumped off my shoulder. And maybe he forgot he couldn't fly or maybe he thought the pot of boiling water was a birdbath. All I know is that he fucking splashed into the water."

"You cooked him?"

"He was only in there a second. I scooped him out with a spoon."

"Where was your daughter?"

"She was right there, and she was screaming like she was burning to death."

"Well, you killed her bird."

"I didn't kill the bird. The bird committed suicide. Attempted suicide. He wasn't dead. He was moving around in my hand. And he was struggling to breathe. And my daughter was screaming at me to save her bird.

And I was trying to figure out how to do CPR on a fucking parakeet."

"So you panicked, then."

"I froze. But my wife was on the phone, calling up the all-night emergency vet place. I mean, man, I didn't even know there was such a thing as an all-night animal ER."

"Did they send an ambulance?"

"Oh, fuck you, you know they didn't send an ambulance. They told us to get that bird into the ER as soon as we could. And so we all piled into my car and busted ass over there."

"Where was the bird?" I ask.

"My wife had it wrapped in a towel on her lap."

"And it survived the ride to the hospital?"

"Tough bird, man. He made it to the hospital. And the doctors took him into the back room and we waited in the waiting room. And my daughter was crying and my wife was crying."

"Were you crying?"

"Yeah, I was bawling like a baby. And there were, like, twenty other people in the waiting room crying for their pets. It was the Waiting Room of the Damned."

"What happened to the bird?"

"He was still alive. The ER doc came out, like it was a fucking movie, and told us the bird was in critical condition and might not make it through the night. So my daughter asks if we could see Harry Potter, and the doc says yes, so he leads us back into the ICU, and we see the bird, and he's hooked up to this tiny little oxygen machine and this tiny little oxygen tube is running down his throat."

"No," I say. I try not to laugh, which makes me laugh. "I'm sorry. I don't mean to laugh. It's not funny."

"Oh, no, that's the whole thing. It *is* funny. It's horrible, too. But it's hilarious at the same time. And when I saw that bird hooked up to those tiny little machines, *I* laughed."

"No."

"Yes, I laughed so hard that I forgot my wife and daughter were standing there. And when I remembered, I turned and looked at them, and they were staring at me with those eyes. Do you know what kind of eyes I'm talking about?"

"Disappointed eyes."

"Yeah, disappointed eyes. But I'm used to those eyes. I mean, I'm married, right? My wife gives me those eyes sixteen times a day. But my daughter was giving me those eyes. And you know what's worse?"

"What?"

"She was ashamed of me. My little girl was ashamed of me. I turned her love and pain into a big fucking laugh."

The man was crying slow tears.

"And then my wife and daughter left me. They got into the car and left me. They went to my mother-in-law's house and they won't talk to me."

"Jesus," I say.

"Christ," he says.

"What happened to the bird?" I asked.

"He died, you stupid shit. You think there's a long list of birds who survive a pot of boiling water? You think God pardons a few parakeets every fucking Memorial Day?"

"I'm sorry," I say.

"You keep your sorrow to yourself," he says.

"Okay."

"Do you feel respected now?" he asks.

"Yes."

"Can I go now?"

"Yes—no, wait," I say. "Do you have a picture?"

"Of the bird?"

"No, of your daughter."

He opens his wallet and shows me a school photo of a pretty little blonde with missing teeth.

"She's great," I say.

"Yeah," he says. "And now she hates me."

"She'll forgive you," I say.

"Do you have any kids?"

That startles me. I don't know this homeless Indian's name, let alone if he has any kids. Does he carry a wallet? I reach into my pockets and find a mess of cards, photos, and receipts fastened with a rubber band.

I snap the rubber band and sort through the mess until I come across a familiar photo.

"Is that your son?" the man asks.

I study the boy's eyes and nose and chin.

"Is that your son?" the man asks again.

"No," I say. "It's me."

"You carry around pictures of yourself?" he asks.

"I don't mean to," I say.

"All right, then," he says. "I'm late for work. I'll see you later."

Without further emotion, the man leaves me. I stare at the photograph. It *is* me, the five-year-old me. The five-year-old Zits. The real me. How did this homeless guy get my photograph? Did my mother send it to him?

I walk over to a delivery truck and turn the side-view mirror. I stare at my bloody reflection. I am older than I used to be. I am battered, bruised, and broken. But I know who I am.

I am my father.

Eighteen

Who can survive such a revelation?

It was father love and father shame and father rage that killed Hamlet. Imagine a new act. Imagine that Hamlet, after being poisoned by his own sword, wakes in the body of his father. Or, worse, inside the body of his incestuous Uncle Claudius?

What would Hamlet do if he looked into the mirror and saw the face of the man who'd betrayed and murdered his father?

And what should I do now that I am looking into the mirror at the face of the man who betrayed and abandoned my mother and me?

If I had a sword, I might slide it into my belly and pull upward until I fell dead, but I have no weapon. And what satisfaction is there in killing a man who wants to die?

All my life, I've been wanting to see my father, to meet him for the first time. I've wanted to ask him questions. To interrogate him.

I stare at his face in the mirror.

"Why did you leave me?" I ask.

He doesn't answer.

"Why do you have a photograph of me when I was five? Did my mother send it to you? Why did you want to carry a photograph of me but not *me*?"

I can feel him fighting me. He doesn't want to remember the day he left me.

But I am younger and stronger. I am better. I will make him remember. I will force him to remember. I will kill him if I have to.

And so I push against my father's mind and soul. I crash through his fortifications and rampage into his memory and tear through his homes, wells, and streets, until I see it: the hospital where I was born. Or, rather, the memory of that hospital. And I burst inside and race up the stairs, and back through the years, and rush through a door into the maternity ward hallway where my father paces.

Somewhere on this floor, my mother is giving birth to me. But my father is not in that room. No, he's outside, removed, remote.

"Sir?" a nurse asks him. "Can I help you?"

"My wife is giving birth," he says.

"Do you know where?"

"Yes, room eight-twelve."

The nurse is confused. Why is he standing here while his wife is giving birth? Men don't wait outside anymore. Men aren't allowed to wait outside anymore. Or maybe there are problems. Maybe it's a difficult birth. Maybe this poor man needs compassion.

"Sir," the nurse says, "your wife and child are going to be okay. We have the finest—"

He puts his hand over her mouth. She doesn't stop him. She's too surprised. Confused. No father has ever touched her face like that. Has violated her boundaries like that. Expectant and fearful fathers have grabbed her. Even pushed or pulled her. But nobody has ever tried to silence her. He realizes his error. He pulls his hand away.

"I'm sorry, I'm sorry," he says. "It's just—I can't stand words right now. I can't stand to hear anybody say anything. Please, just go. Just go and leave me alone."

She quickly walks away, wonders briefly if she should call security, but then realizes that the man has enough problems. She knows he's just a weak man ashamed of his weakness.

She prays for him. Dear God, she thinks, help this man become a better man than he is now.

My father doesn't feel her prayers.

He only feels a sharp pain in his chest. Something has broken. He knows he is sick and damaged. But what has made him sick? And what has damaged him?

My father remembers being eight years old, lying in bed while a man stands in the dark doorway. Who is that man?

It is my father's father.

"I know you're awake," my grandfather says. He is drunk, slurs his words, and wavers in the doorway.

My father doesn't move. He believes that his father will go away if he doesn't move. It's a magic spell that gets repeated every Friday and Saturday night.

"Your momma said you went out shooting today," Grandfather says.

When my father hunts, he imagines the animals, the targets, are his father.

"Did you bring down anything?" Grandfather asks.

My father imagines pressing the rifle barrel against my grandfather's temple. Imagines pulling the trigger.

"Did you kill anything? Any meat?" Grandfather asks.

That day, my father shot at and missed three quail and one deer.

"I asked you if you got any meat," Grandfather says.

My father doesn't want to tell the truth. The truth will get him hurt. A lie will also get him hurt. He's going to get hurt no matter what he does.

"If you don't answer my question, boy, I'm gonna get mad."

Silence.

"I'm gonna ask you one more time," Grandfather says. "Did you shoot anything today?"

"No," my father says.

"Jesus," Grandfather says. "What good are you? What kind of man are you? Ain't I taught you how to shoot? And you waste my time and my bullets and my energy. You're just a pussy boy. I can't believe you are part of me. I wish you'd just go away."

And then my grandfather leaves my father alone in the dark.

My father wants to weep. He wants to cry out for his father. He wants to be forgiven, to be loved. But if he speaks he will only be ridiculed again. He will only be diminished.

And then my grandfather walks back into the room. He stands over my father.

"I want you to know what I know," my grandfather says. "You ain't worth shit now. And you ain't ever gonna be worth shit."

My father stares at a stain on the ceiling. He has memorized the shape of that stain.

"Say it," my grandfather says.

"Say what?" my father asks.

"Say you ain't worth shit."

My father wants to resist, to rebel, but he knows the punishment will end only if he submits.

"I ain't worth shit," my father says.

"Say it again."

"I ain't worth shit."

"Louder."

"I ain't worth shit!" my father screams.

"Louder."

"I ain't worth shit!" my father screams. "I ain't worth shit! I ain't worth shit! I ain't worth shit! I ain't worth shit!"

My father screams long after my grandfather has left the room.

And now my father, whipped and bloodied by his memory, stops pacing in the hospital hallway. Somewhere on this floor, my mother is giving birth to me. But my father cannot be a participant. He cannot be a witness. He cannot be a father.

And so he runs. And as he runs, he closes his eyes. And as he closes his eyes, I close my eyes.

Nineteen

When I open my eyes, I'm standing in a bank in downtown Seattle.

Yes, that bank.

I have two pistols in my coat, a paint gun and a .38
special.

Yes, those guns.

I'm supposed to pull them out and shoot everybody
I see.

Yes, I'm supposed to kill for Justice.

I did it before: a long time ago, a little while ago,
a second ago. I don't understand how time works
anymore.

There's that man again, the one who told me I wasn't
real.

I think he's wrong; I think I am real.

I have returned to my body. And my ugly face. And my anger. And my loneliness.

And then I think, Maybe I never left my body at all. Maybe I never left this bank. Maybe I've been standing here for hours, minutes, seconds, trying to decide what I should do.

Do I pull out my guns and shoot all these people?

Do I shoot that little boy over there with his mother? He is maybe five years old. He has blue eyes and blond hair. He's wearing good shoes. A jean jacket. Khaki pants. Blue shirt. He's beautiful. A beautiful little man. His mother, also blond and blue-eyed, smiles down at him. She loves him. She sees me watching them and she smiles at me. For me. She wants me to know how much she loves her son. She's proud of the little guy.

Did my mother love me like that? I hope so.

I wave at the little boy. He waves back.

I hate him for being loved so well.

I want to be him.

I close my eyes and try to step inside his body. But it doesn't work. I cannot be him.

I open my eyes. I think all the people in this bank are better than I am. They have better lives than I do. Or maybe they don't. Maybe we're all lonely. Maybe some of them also hurtle through time and see war, war, war. Maybe we're all in this together.

I turn around and walk out of the bank. I step out onto First Avenue.

It's not really raining, but this is Seattle. There are only fifty-eight sunny days a year in our city. So it always feels like it's just about to rain, even when the sun is out.

I used to hate the rain. But now I want it to pour. I want it to storm. I want to be clean.

I am surrounded by people who trust me to be a respectful stranger. Am I trustworthy? Are any of us trustworthy? I hope so.

I remember my first day of school. Kindergarten. My mother walked me there. It was only six blocks away from our apartment, but six blocks is forever to a child.

As we walked, my mother talked to me.

"It's going to be okay," she said. "School is a good thing. You're going to have lots of friends. And you'll learn so much. And the teachers will take care of you, okay? I love you, okay? You'll be okay. I'm going to wait right here for you. All day, I'll wait right here."

She was wrong, of course. School was not good for me.

I never made friends.

I didn't learn much.

I was not okay.

And my mother didn't wait for me. She died.

After she died, I went to live with her sister, my aunt.

Yes, that's the dirtiest secret I own.

This is what I don't tell anybody. I don't talk about it. I don't dream about it. I don't want anybody to know.

My aunt was supposed to take care of me. She had

hurt.

I need help.

I walk from street to street, looking for help. I walk past Pike Place Market and Nordstrom's. I walk past Gameworks and the Space Needle. I walk past Lake Washington and Lake Union. I walk for miles. I walk for days. I walk for years.

I don't understand how time works anymore.

I walk until I see a police car parked in front of a restaurant.

I walk inside.

It's a cheap diner. Eight tables. Two waitresses. A cook in the back.

At one of the tables sit two cops, Officer Dave and his partner. They've arrested me more often than any other duo.

I walk up to them.

"Officer Dave," I say.

"Hey, Zits," he says. "What's going on?"

I want to tell him the entire story. I want to tell him that I fell through time and have only now returned. I want to tell him I learned a valuable lesson. But I don't know what that lesson is. It's too complicated, too strange. Or maybe it really is simple. Maybe it's so simple it makes me feel stupid to say it.

Maybe you're not supposed to kill. No matter who tells you to do it. No matter how good or bad the reason. Maybe you're supposed to believe that all life is sacred.

"Officer Dave," I say, and raise my hands high in the air, "I want you to know that I respect you. And I'm here for a good reason. I'm raising my hands up because I have two guns inside my coat. One of them is just a paint gun, but the other one is real."

Officer Dave and his partner quickly get to their feet. Their hands touch their guns, ready to pull them out of their holsters.

"This isn't funny, Zits," Officer Dave says. "You say stuff like that, you're going to get shot."

I start laughing.

"What's so funny?" Officer Dave asks.

"I'm not trying to be funny," I say. "And I don't want to get shot. I really do have two guns. I want you to take them from me. Please, take them away."

Twenty

Officer Dave takes my guns.

And then he takes me to the police station. He stands nearby as a detective interviews me. He's a big black man with big eyeglasses. He calls it an interview. It's really an interrogation. I don't mind. I guess I deserve to be interrogated.

"Where did you get the guns?" Detective Eyeglasses asks.

"I got them from a kid named Justice," I say.

"Was Justice his first or last name?"

"He just called himself Justice. That's all. He said he gave himself the name."

"You don't know his real name?"

"No."

"Where did you meet him?"

"In jail."

"When was this?"

"A few months ago, I guess. Don't really remember. I've been in jail a lot."

"Okay, so you met him in jail. But you don't remember exactly when. And you say his name is Justice. But that's not his real name."

"Yeah."

"None of that information helps us much, does it? It's not very specific, is it?"

"No, I guess not."

I can tell that Detective Eyeglasses doesn't believe me. He thinks I invented Justice.

"You say this guy named Justice is the one who told you to go to the bank and kill people?" Eyeglasses asks me.

"Yeah," I say.

The detective stares at me hard, like his eyes were twin suns. I feel burned.

He pulls a TV cart into the room and plays a video for me. It's a copy of the bank security tape.

Eyeglasses, Officer Dave, and I watch a kid named Zits walk into the bank and stand near a huge potted plant.

I laugh.

"What's so funny?" Eyeglasses asks.

"I just look stupid next to that big plant. Look at me, I'm trying to hide behind it."

It's true. I'm using it for cover. Eyeglasses and Officer Dave have to laugh, too. It is funny. But it's only funny because I didn't do what I was supposed to do. It's only funny because I'm alive to watch it. It's only funny because everybody in that bank is still alive.

So maybe it's not really funny at all.

Maybe we're all laughing because it's so fucking unfunny.

In the video, I pat my coat once, twice, three times.

"What are you doing?" Eyeglasses asks.

"I'm checking to see if my guns are still there," I say.

"Are you thinking about using them?"

"Yeah."

"But you didn't. Why not?"

On the video, my image disappears for a second. I'm gone. And then I reappear.

"Whoa," Officer Dave says. "Did you see that?"

The detective rewinds the tape. Presses PLAY. I'm there in the bank. Then I'm gone—*poof.* And then I reappear.

"That's weird," Officer Dave says.

"Aw, it's just a flaw in the tape," Eyeglasses says. "They reuse these tapes over and over. The quality goes down. They got weird bumps and cuts in them."

Eyeglasses is probably right.

On the video, I am staring at the little blond boy and his mother. I smile and wave.

"Who is that?" Eyeglasses asks me.

"It's just a boy and his mother," I say.

"Do you know them?"

"No."

"Then why are you being so friendly to them?"

"They were beautiful," I say.

Detective Eyeglasses snorts at me. He thinks I'm goofy. But Officer Dave smiles. He must be a father.

"Do you know where we might find this Justice?" Eyeglasses asks me.

"Maybe," I say. "We lived together in this warehouse down in SoDo."

"Jesus," he says. "Why didn't you tell us this before?"

"You didn't ask."

I lead them to the warehouse. I wait outside with two rookie cops while Dave and Eyeglasses and a SWAT team check out the whole building.

Nobody is there.

Pretty soon, Eyeglasses comes out and takes me upstairs to the room where Justice and I lived for a few weeks.

There are empty cans, bottles, and plastic containers. There are two beds made out of newspaper and cardboard. There are newspaper photos and magazine articles taped on the walls. All the people in those photos and articles have crosshairs painted over their faces. They were all targets.

"This is where you and Justice lived?" Eyeglasses asks me.

"Yeah."

"Well, if he was here, he's gone now."

"Yeah."

I know that I won't see Justice again.

Eyeglasses stares at me hard. He's good at staring hard.

"Zits," he says. "I'm happy you changed your mind about using those guns."

I'm happy, too, but I can't say that.

Later, as I sit in a holding cell, waiting for a transfer to yet another halfway house or juvie hall or real prison, Officer Dave visits me.

He leans against the bars of my cell.

"You're going to die," he says.

I'm trying to be as tough as I used to be, but it's not working. I feel like a carton of eggs holding up an elephant.

"You are going to die," Dave says again. He says each syllable like it was a cussword. Or a prayer.

"So I'm going to die," I say. "What does it matter? I don't matter. I'm nothing."

"Zits," he says. "You matter. Everybody matters. You matter to me."

"You're a cop," I say. "You don't care about anything."

"I care too much, man," Dave says.

I look at him. Tears are rolling down his big cop face. Who knew that cops could cry?

"What's wrong with you?" I ask.

Dave wipes his face. He's embarrassed by his tears. But he has something important to say, so he says it.

"A few weeks ago, we got this nine-one-one call," he tells me. "A man said there was this crazy screaming in the house next door. Like babies just crying and crying, louder than he ever heard before."

Dave looks at the ceiling as if his memory was playing like a movie up there. I look up and see it, too.

I can't jump into Dave's body but I can feel and see and understand a little bit about his pain, I guess.

In their squad car, Dave and his partner pull up in front of a house. A small, dirty house. Garbage on the lawn. Two broken cars in the driveway.

The cops knock on the front door.

No answer.

They knock.

No answer.

Dave puts his ear to the door.

"Can you hear that?" he asks.

"What is it?" his partner asks.

"It sounds like water running."

Dave steps down on the lawn and peers through the front window. Through a crack in the curtains, he can see two people lying on the floor.

"Two people down, two people down," he says.

Dave and his partner draw their guns and burst through the front door.

Two people lying on the living room floor. A man and a woman. Dead.

No, alive: passed out.

Beer bottles, wine bottles, vodka bottles, crack pipes, the stink of meth.

"Jesus, I hate that smell," the partner says. He kicks the man. "Wake up," he says.

The man doesn't move. Just breathes heavy.

He kicks the man again. Harder. "Wake the fuck up," he says.

The man just lies there.

"I hate these freaks," the partner says.

But Dave is already moving into another room. He's following that sound: running water. He steps into a pool of water in the hallway.

Cold water. Where's it coming from? The bathroom at the end of the hallway.

"We got something going on here," Dave says to his partner.

Together, they walk down the hallway. Through the water. Getting deeper. Flooding the house.

They reach the bathroom door.

With head nods and hand signals, they talk to each other.

Are you ready to go in?

Yes.

Okay, on three.

One, two, three.

Dave turns the knob and pushes against the door.

It's locked.

No, it's just stuck. A difficult door. Dave pushes hard. The door screeches open.

And they see two toddlers, a boy and a girl, two or three years old, lying still on the floor.

Covered with burns: their legs, their backs, their bellies.

Hot-water scalds.

The tub faucet pours out water. Overfills the tub. Floods the room.

It's cold water now. Ice cold. But it was boiling hot when it overflowed the tub, when the two babies were trapped by the difficult door, when they screamed so loud that the neighbor could hear them, but not so loud that it woke their parents from their drunken stoned slumber.

"Oh, my God! Oh . . . my . . . God!" Dave shouts. "Get an ambulance here, now, now, now!"

Dave's partner calls for help.

Dave kneels down in the water and picks up the babies, one in each arm. Their eyes are open and blue and blind. They're gone.

Dave cries.

He wants to go back in time. He only needs to travel back an hour—just one hour—and he'll be able to save these kids. He'll take them away from their terrible parents, from this terrible life, and he'll love them. He'll keep them safe.

"They were just babies," Dave says to me. "Helpless little babies. I couldn't save them. I was too late."

I don't know what to say.

Dave weeps. I weep with him.

He leans against the bars of my cell. I don't know if I'm the one in jail, or if he is.

Twenty-one

After months of counseling, social work, mental therapy, and absolute boredom, the medical professionals and social workers and cops decide that I am not going to kill anybody. I am not dangerous.

Really, that's what they say to me: "Zits, we don't think you're dangerous."

How am I supposed to respond to something like that?

"Oh, uh, thank you, ma'am."

I mean, jeez, I'm a fifteen-year-old foster kid with a history of fire setting, time traveling, body shifting, and mass-murder contemplation. I think I'm a lot more than just dangerous.

I think I might be unlovable.

But as dangerous and unlovable as I am, the state places me in a temporary foster home.

With Officer Dave's brother and sister-in-law.

"They don't have any kids," Officer Dave says. "But they always wanted a baby."

I don't think I exactly qualify as a bouncing baby boy, but who am I to complain?

"Is your brother a cop?" I ask.

"He's a fireman," Dave says. "My other brother works for the post office."

"Jesus," I say. "You guys are like the civil servant hall of fame or something."

Dave laughs. I always could make him laugh. I hope I can make his brother laugh.

Man, I can't believe that a firefighter is going to be my new foster father, but it does make some kind of metaphorical sense, doesn't it?

I guess they really want me to be under close supervision. Well, I'm happy it's only going to be temporary. I'll go crazy living with a firefighter. They always walk around looking for smoke.

I want to ask Dave why he's sending me to his brother. Why doesn't Dave just take care of me by himself? I think I know the answer. I think he's scared of disappointing me.

The social workers deliver me to the firefighter's house in the middle of the night, like some sort of major-league prisoner or something. They don't have me in handcuffs, but I feel handcuffed, if you know what I mean.

They put me in this little bedroom. And I lie there in the dark and wonder if I can fall asleep in a strange bed. But I fall asleep while worrying that I might not fall asleep.

The alarm clock wakes me up at 7 A.M. It plays Blood, Sweat & Tears. Really.

That song called "I Love You More Than You Will Ever Know." The one my mother used to sing to me.

It makes me want to gag. How cruel is this? I'm living in a firefighter's house and the alarm plays my mother's favorite song.

I turn off the music, go into the bathroom, and pee for two minutes.

Then I walk out into the kitchen.

Officer Dave is eating breakfast with his brother and sister-in-law: oatmeal and fruit and sausage. It smells great. Dave and the firefighter are wearing their uniforms. The wife is wearing a nurse's uniform. And she's kind of hot, you know. She's really tall and has long brown hair and brown eyes. Her cheekbones are big, too, like Indian cheekbones. I wonder if she's a little bit Indian. She smells pretty great, too. She smells even better than the oatmeal, fruit, and sausage.

"Good morning," she says to me. "Do you want some oatmeal?"

"Whatever," I say, and sit down.

The firefighter looks at me. He's not reading a newspaper. He's not ignoring me. He looks right at me.

"My name is Robert," he says and offers his hand. I take it. We shake like gentlemen.

Officer Dave stares at me, too. I think he's thinking about those two babies in the bathroom. I wonder if he'll always look at me and see those two babies in the bathroom. I hope not. I hope someday he looks at me and just sees me.

"Hey, Zits," he says. "After work today, I'm thinking all of us men should go to the Mariners game. What do you think?"

I want to say Whatever, but it doesn't come out that way. I realize that Dave isn't leaving me to his brother. Dave is going to take care of me, too. That makes sense, I suppose. I need as many fathers as possible.

"You ever been to a baseball game?" Robert asks me.

"I've never seen one in person," I say.

A baseball game! Jesus, how American. Next thing you know, Dave and the firefighter and I will be playing catch in the backyard.

"Well, I got some tickets," Dave says.

"They're shitty seats," Robert says. "My brother is a cheap-ass bastard. We're going to be way up in the sky. Behind home plate. But they're fun anyway. We'll watch the game and eat hot dogs and drink lemonade. How does that sound?"

Before I can answer, his wife speaks up.

"You will not eat junk," she says. "I'll pack you some fruits and vegetables. And you'll drink water. Lots of water."

She smiles at me. Her teeth are the brightest teeth in the world. Every one of those teeth is a statue of somebody beautiful.

"My name is Mary," she says. "I'm happy you're here with us."

"It's only temporary," I say.

"Well, Robert and I are hoping to make it permanent," she says. "How does that sound to you?"

For a second, I can't even remember what that word means. For a moment, I forget that the word *permanent* ever existed.

"Wow," I say. "Permanent might be pretty cool."

I look at Dave. He's smiling. How often do cops smile? Not very much, I guess, because Dave's smile is goofy and big. If he knew how goofy and big it was, he'd practice more.

He's trying to save me. And he's smiling about it. I guess that's okay. Maybe I can save him, too.

"Okay, kid," he says. "We got to go. I'll see you back here after work."

Robert kisses Mary and leaves. Dave tousles my hair and leaves. Yes, he tousles my hair. No father has tousled a kid's hair since 1955. I wonder if I have dropped into some weird time-travel thing again. But no, Dave is just a decent guy. Wow.

So I'm here alone with Mary. I'm in love.

Is it okay to be in love with your foster mother? Well, to be honest, I don't care if it's okay or not.

"All right," she says. "After breakfast, I'm going to take you down to the new school and get you enrolled. And then I'm going to work for a few hours. And then I'll come back and pick you up after, okay?"

She's giving me a schedule.

"What time will you pick me up?" I ask.

"Well," she says. "School gets out at two-thirty. So I'll meet you in front about two-forty-five. How does that sound?"

"Are you really going to be there?" I ask.

She smiles, but there's a little sadness in her eyes, too. She knows I've been lied to a million times.

"I'll be there," she says. "I promise."

Promise. What a good word. What a hopeful word.

"Whatever," I say, because it hurts to have hope.

"Hey, listen," she says, and leans down close to me. Her face is three inches from mine. She looks right into my eyes. "When I make promises, I keep them. Do you understand?"

"Yes," I say.

"Do you believe me?"

"Yes," I say. And you know what's weird? I *do* believe her.

"All right, then," she says. "Finish your breakfast."

So I eat until my belly is stuffed and then I go into my bathroom to get ready.

I have my own bathroom!

Pretty soon there's a knock on the door.

"Yes," I say.

"Can I come in?" she asks.

"Yeah, I'm decent," I say, and laugh. I've never been decent, not once. And I've never used that word before. I'm getting soft.

Mary comes in. She looks a little nervous. She's carrying a bag of stuff.

"Is there something wrong?" I ask.

"No," she says. "It's just—well, this is difficult. But can I say something really personal to you?"

"Okay, I guess."

"Well, it's about your face."

"I know. I'm ugly."

"No, you're not ugly. You're handsome, actually. But your skin—we need to start working on your skin. You'll be a lot happier if we do."

She reaches into the bag and pulls out three jars and sets them on the sink.

"Okay," she says. "This is some skin-care treatment stuff, okay? I'm going to teach you how to use it, okay?"

"Okay," I say.

"Well, first of all, you need to wash your face with this stuff. It's an acne scrub. It will clean your pores and get rid of the old dead skin, okay?"

"Okay," I say, and wash my face.

"Good, good," she says. "Then we use this stuff to put right on your pimples. This goes after the bacteria in there. So just put a little on your fingertip and dab it on the big zits, okay?"

That takes me awhile. I have a lot of zits.

"Okay, good," she says. "Now this last stuff, it's an all-over moisturizer and oil-reducing cream. It's funny, but it will keep your skin moist but dry at the same time."

"I don't get it," I say.

"I don't either," she says, "but it works, okay? Trust me."

I rub that stuff all over my face.

"There, that's good," she says. "We do this twice a day, and your face should start clearing up in a week or two. A few months from now, you'll be brand-new."

That just gets me in the soul. Right there, I start to cry. Really. I just weep and wail.

Mary hugs me. She hugs me tightly. It feels great. I haven't been hugged like that since my mother died.

I'm happy.

I'm scared, too. I mean, I know the world is still a cold and cruel place.

I know that people will always go to war against each other.

I know that children will always be targets.

I know that people will always betray each other.

I know that I am a betrayer.

But I'm beginning to think I've been given a chance. I'm beginning to think I might get unlonely. I'm beginning to think I might have an almost real family.

"I'm sorry, I'm sorry, I'm sorry," I keep saying.

"It's okay," she says. "You'll be okay."

"Michael," I say. "My real name is Michael. Please, call me Michael."

Acknowledgments

I owe special thanks to Nancy Stauffer, for her continuing grace and friendship; to Morgan, Elisabeth, Deb, Eric, and everybody else at Grove, who were there in the beginning and are still with me in the middle; to Christy Cox, who keeps order in my insane life; and to my mother and siblings, who let me write about them and don't complain publicly.

FLIGHT

Sherman Alexie

A BLACK CAT READING GUIDE
PREPARED BY BARBARA PUTNAM

ABOUT THIS GUIDE

We hope that these discussion questions
will enhance your reading group's exploration
of Sherman Alexie's *Flight*. They are
meant to stimulate discussion, offer new viewpoints,
and enrich your enjoyment of the book.

More reading group guides and additional information,
including summaries, author tours, and author sites,
for other fine Black Cat titles, may be found on
our Web site, www.groveatlantic.com.

FLIGHT

Sherman Alexie

A BLACK CAT READING GUIDE

QUESTIONS FOR DISCUSSION

1. The narrator begins the novel by stating, "My zits are me," defining himself by his affliction. How else does he define himself? Speculating about rock stars with "stringy hair and greasy beards and bloodshot eyes," Zits says, "As ugly as I am, I might have been the biggest rock star in the world" (p. 2). How, as he learns in juvenile detention (p. 26), is the acne a badge both of shame and poverty? How does his identity begin to change in the book? Does he seem liberated by inhabiting clean-faced people in his travels?

2. How is shame at the heart of dislocated Indians? What kinds of shame, besides his "ugliness," does Zits suffer from? (see p. 5). How does the physical stigma serve as a metaphor for larger cultural deprivations? For the human condition? Can you think of other figures in literature for whom one oddity or deformity is emblematic of greater dilemmas? One thinks of Kafka's Gregor in *Metamorphosis* who awakens one day as a giant, awkward insect. Or Captain Ahab with his cursed wooden leg in *Moby-Dick*. Others?

3. Zits has had twenty foster families by the time he is fifteen, and he started running away from them at age eight. What is the picture of foster parents he conveys in the

book? Have you found that view corroborated in newspaper articles? "When it comes to foster parents, there are only two kinds: the good but messy people who are trying to help kids or the absolute welfare vultures that like to cash government checks every month. . . . But who cares, right? It's not like I'm going to be here much longer. I'm never in any one place long enough to care" (p. 8). Do you see that Zits might have done things differently to make some of these foster homes work better?

4. "Whatever" is his protective shield, and sometimes his weapon, to straight-arm people who might get too close to him or make demands. Does he make you think of Holden Caulfield in his teenage alienation? Anyone else?

5. "My mother loved me more than any of you will ever know" (p. 3). Is this the boy's talisman? Is it the core of him that might ultimately provide a way out of his cycling nightmares, real and imagined? He also thinks his mother got cancer from grieving at her loss of his father. How did his own grief make him even more vulnerable to the repeated abuses of his childhood?

6. Zits is a boy whose childhood was taken away from him, leaving him bleakly lonely. "I don't know any other Native Americans, except the homeless Indians who wander around downtown Seattle. . . . Of course, those wandering Indians are not the only Indians in the world, but they're the only ones who pay attention to me" (p. 7). One thinks, too, of the drunken street Indian later in the book who shouts that he needs some respect. Are there ways to reclaim the lives of down-and-outers? Zits scoffs at the "overeducated, yoga-addicted" social worker who urges him to wear a necktie and shine his shoes to develop "a sense of citizenship" and learn to be a "fully realized human being" (pp. 6-7). Do you think the visible outward signs of uniforms in certain inner-city schools contribute

to law, order, and self-respect? Should neckties and shoe-shine kits be part of shelters?

7. Among many sad, bitter, angry, vengeful characters in Zits's life and travels are several who stand out for their humanity. Think about people who risk their lives for strangers, such as Little Saint and even Gus, the white liberals in Spokane, and Dave who as a good cop puts his life on the line every day, even before he and Mary take the huge risk they do at the end. Are there others you can think of? Does Zits take stands that put him in this category?

8. As in *The Glass Castle* by Jeanette Walls, we are startled to read about people rummaging through Dumpsters for food just to survive, even in this land of great plenty. Zits says, "I hate my country. There are so many rich people who don't share. . . . They're like spoiled little ten-year-old bullies on the playground . . . if you try to get even one spin on the merry-go-round, the bullies beat the shit out of you" (p. 26). Do you see any of this in your community?

9. Justice picks his own name. "But I wish I'd been given my name by Indians. You guys used to give out names because people earned them" (p. 30). Zits is burdened not only with his spots but also with the rather horrible name. Yet Officer Dave can say it with growing affection. Does the last line of the book represent a name the boy hopes to earn? A state of grace perhaps?

10. What is the myth of the Ghost Dance? How does it create a dilemma for this boy of mixed blood? (see pp. 31–34). How does the myth relate to the bank scene where Zits takes his two pistols?

11. "I turn around to look at myself in the mirror. I expect to see me pretending to be Clint Eastwood. But instead I am looking at a face that is not my own" (p. 40). Fantasy?

Nightmare? How do you read this dramatic down-the-rabbit hole book? It is a novel but also memoir, science fiction, travel literature, thriller, political polemic, and cri-de-coeur. Talk about these fused elements of Alexie's work.

12. Whether it's Teddy Roosevelt or FBI agents, the outside perception of Indians is not positive. "None of them is worth much. Well, maybe some of the kids . . . are still okay. But they're going to go bad, too. Just you watch. There's something bad inside these Indians. They can't help themselves" (p. 45). It's a cliché that Indians will "go bad," drink and fight on the streets . . . a sad departure from the idea of the noble savage (which has its own problems of misperception). How does Zits have to work through not only the myth but also the reality of this negative image?

13. What do we learn about 1975 Indian history in the story of Hank and Art, Hammer and Iron in Chapters 4, 5, and 6? What is the irony of Horse and Elk's being regarded as heroes—back in the future?

14. Did you find a disconnect between the treacherous acts of Horse and Elk and their subsequent urgency about a traditional, decent burial for the sacrificed Junior? Were you reminded of Sophocles's Antigone, whose family custom and her gods required dignified burial for her brother even though he had been killed as a traitor, and burial was forbidden by the king? Here we see Indian traitors, themselves responsible for the death who yet insist on taking responsibility for carrying out a ceremony. Do some of the Mafia stories resonate here?

15. When Art dismisses Hank's concerns about the murder of Junior, he says (through tears he ignores), "We're at war. We're soldiers. And soldiers have to do some tough things. . . . And some of the things we have to do, they hurt us,

you know? They hurt us inside. . . . In order to fight evil, sometimes we have to do evil things" (p. 56). Is there something chilling about this rhetoric from an FBI agent? Does this section make us think further about the consequences of war, to both captors and the captured? "Art and Justice fight on opposite sides of the war but they sound exactly like each other. How can you tell the difference between the good guys and the bad guys when they say the same things?" (p. 56). Discuss these rationalizations of Art. Any thoughts about the world today?

16. What are the ways Zits can feel powerful? Is that part of his quest? Think of Justice and his pair of guns. And Hank's wife's kisses: "God, I think I would kill for her kiss" (p. 58). Other ways?

17. Throughout his time travels and body jumping, Zits retains a sense of himself. What narrative purpose might this serve? Consider his response to violence: the torture of an Indian detainee on the 1975 reservation, for instance. How does Hank/Zits respond? Thinking back that he has killed a crowd of people in the bank, Zits realizes "I am Hank Storm, too" (p. 52). These killers of Indians are not *other*, he thinks. Hank Storm is his double. What does Alexie achieve by this sleight-of-hand? When Hank is ordered to reshoot Junior, the sense of connection is redoubled. "Scared, I pull out my pistol and stand over Junior's body. He looks so young. He's a kid. Like me . . . Justice made all this killing make sense. But it doesn't make sense, does it? I'm going crazy. I am crazy" (p. 53). How does Zits react to violence in his other time-travel roles?

18. How would you describe Alexie's style? Edgy, energetic? Imaginative? Surreal? Does he make you think of Dalí or Magritte, with their sense of nonsense? He captures dream-like leaps and disjunctures that still provide an odd logic. "I'm running through the dark. I run toward the sound of laugh-

ter. I run toward a bright light in the distance. I run super fast. And I wonder if I'm not running at all. What if I'm flying? What if I have become that bank guard's bullet? What if I'm the bullet that blasted through my brain?" (p. 59). Does it sound like peoples' description of near-death experiences? Zits says earlier, "I used to dream that I could run fast enough to burn up like a meteor and drop little pieces of me all over the world" (p. 16). Is that an image of what happens to him in his time travel? What are other aspects of Alexie's style in this book?

19. "I suddenly burst through the bright light, which is really the opening of a buffalo-skin tepee, and I run outside and stop. I am standing in the middle of a gigantic Indian camp. And I don't mean some Disneyland, Nickelodeon, roller-coaster, stuffed-animal, cotton-candy Indian camp. Nope" (p. 59). Zits offers this disclaimer but how trustworthy is this narrator? After all, he said earlier that all he learned about Indians, champion-level Indian Trivial Pursuit knowledge, he learned from television. Is this the stuff of dreams? "These are how Indians are supposed to be" (p. 60). By whose lights? Even today Indians gather for giant powwows, as in Taos. These festivals are for tourism, certainly, but are they also a lifeline for retaining a culture and passing it on in tribes? What are your thoughts about assimilation as opposed to fighting for strong cultural traditions? Not only in Indians but also in other groups, including immigrants?

20. "These old-time Indians have dark skin. There aren't any half-breed pale beige green-eyed Indians here. Nope, unlike me, these Indians are the real deal" (p. 60). Do you think intermarriage and watering down of bloodlines necessarily deprives people of authenticity? Zits has been robbed not only of a childhood but a sense of being Indian, except in a pejorative way. Do you think it is ludicrous that even though federal regulations state that Indian children

should be placed in Indian foster homes, because his father never legitimized his paternity, Zits falls between those regulatory stools, too? And since his mother died when he was six, he didn't absorb Irishness either. Have you read about other mixed-blood people in this melting-pot country who had to work on discovering roots and authenticity and a sense of self? Think of Barak Obama and *Search for My Father*, in which he retraces his white upbringing and subsequent efforts to understand and participate in the black experience, including an odyssey to Kenya, the land of his birth father. If feeling of loss or confusion can be overcome, is it possible that intermarriage, whether race or religion, can produce people of broadened vision, with insights from both worlds? Talk about these ideas. (Later, Zits as Indian boy, sees Crazy Horse. "I think the greatest warrior in Sioux history is a half-breed mystery. I think this legendary killer of white men *is* half-white, like me" (p. 68). Is this a wedge of understanding that there might be a valid place for a half-breed like himself?)

21. Quite apart from his original acne, Zits acquires other disabilities as the book progresses. In the Indian camp, what happens to the boy (another of Zits's doubles) when his warrior father picks him up and hugs him? It is a moment he has longed for, back in the future, for fifteen years. How does he respond? He wants to scream "Daddy," but he can't make a sound. Is this some archetypal dream terror? "I reach up, touch my throat, and feel a huge fleshy knot. It's on my voice box. I don't know if I was attacked by a person or by a disease, but my voice has been taken away" (p. 64). From what other impairments do his doubles suffer? Is this metaphor something unique to Zits, or to Indians, or to abused children, or are they manifestations of flaws or burdens we all bear?

22. This Indian boy of the nineteenth century retains his knowledge of the tribes' future. What can he do with this

tragic vision? What other genocidal sweeps are you reminded of? "They'll be packed into train cars and shipped off to reservations. And they'll starve in winter camps near iced-over rivers" (p. 66). Do you think that here Alexie has expanded his myth of Native Americans into something more universal? "The children are going to be kidnapped and sent off to boarding schools. Their hair will be cut short and they will be beaten for speaking the tribal languages. They'll be beaten for dancing and singing the old-time Indian songs" (p. 66). How do you respond to the complicated symbolism of Indians today getting rich from casinos . . . as they fleece mostly white people? Is this corruption of all concerned, or do the Indians deserve this chance at reclamation if not retribution?

23. In *Flight* do you sense a dreadful inevitability about the path of Native Americans? "All of them are going to start drinking booze. And their children will drink booze. . . . And one of those grandchildren will grow up to be my real father, the one who decided that drinking booze was more important than being my father. The one who abandoned my mother and me" (p. 67). What is suggested in the novel about a way out of the terrible cycle?

24. How is the spirit of myth, of universal truths, evoked by the events along the Little Bighorn? Crazy Horse, Sitting Bull, and of course, Custer. About Crazy Horse: "The magical one. Bullets couldn't hit him. He could never be photographed. He was a holy ghost, the Sioux Jesus" (p. 68). How does Alexie create immediacy, putting us right on the scene? "Daddy! Daddy! This is the camp at Little Bighorn! Custer is coming! Custer is coming! He's bringing the Seventh Cavalry and they're coming to kill us! . . . But of course I cannot actually say anything because I don't have a working voice box" (p. 68). Is he something between a mute Chicken Little and a Cassandra who wants to warn, but no one hears?

25. How is Custer portrayed in Chapter 9? Is this the conventional picture of him, or has he been romanticized as a defender of the white man? In *Flight* we learn "He wanted all the glory for himself" (p. 71). Despite the poetic justice of crushing defeat for the rash, vainglorious general, how does Alexie still force us to see the ambiguities and plain horrors of war? Think of the Indian victors' celebrations and the grandmothers' brutal vengeance; the anger and lust for revenge goes that deep. As Alexie debunks part of the Indian myth, does he also universalize the frequent viciousness of victory?

26. Rites of passage around the world are often violent, for both boys and girls. Discuss examples. What does the Indian boy's warrior father expect of him . . . or offer him? "He's just a kid, like me. I didn't know they let kids join the cavalry" (p. 74). What is the connection between his scarred throat and his father's implacable lust for revenge? How does the boy/Zits try to understand by recalling his rich white foster father (one of twenty, remember) who had the basement train collection? Why does the scene end before the boy actually cuts the soldier's throat? Is there a gradual de-escalation of violence on Zits's part as the book goes on?

27. Is it true that from the playing fields to battle grounds, fathers, coaches, drill sergeants, and politicians are often urging boys to be men, aggressive men? "My father yells at me in his language. He wants me to be a warrior. I am only a child. . . . I stare at the white soldier in front of me. . . . He's a child and I'm a child, and I'm supposed to slash his throat. What do I do? I close my eyes" (p. 78). Talk about these problems, not new to our time.

28. Is the time journey more nightmare than mythical quest? At least in the *Odyssey,* besides his monsters and vengeful gods, Odysseus has idyllic and seductive moments. Such moments are fleeting at best in this story. "I guess I must be a soldier

now. I wonder which war I'm going to be fighting" (p. 80). How are the wars he endures or observes different from and similar to each other?

29. What are possible explanations for Zits's travels back in time? Is it more than time travel? He actually inhabits these other beings. Is it guilt—from the bank adventure? Is it empathy that makes him assume these other identities?

30. What ties these stories together? How does the journey of Zits begin to cohere? War, vengeance, and power are clearly under scrutiny. As are treachery and infidelity. The brutality is atrocious as the white soldiers slaughter Indian warriors and a camp of women and children. Do we feel caught in an endless nightmare? One that reflects many parts of our world today? "But, no . . . Wait . . . Carrying an Indian child, a white soldier is running with Indians. . . . In the midst of all this madness and murder, one soldier has refused to participate. He has chosen the opposite of revenge. Somehow that one white boy, that small saint, has held on to a good and kind heart. A courageous and beautiful heart" (p. 93). How does this man's action change the way Zits acts in his doubles' bodies?

31. What is the reward of a kind heart in Small Saint? What war stories like this can you remember? Refusal to commit violence punished as treason. Are we hearing analogous stories about members of the U.S. military who go AWOL or refuse to serve?

32. Zits often ends his adventures or escapes by falling asleep. In Shakespeare this is often a chance to rest, dream, and awaken to rebirth. Does it work that way in *Flight*? Talk about the circumstances that precede his falling asleep in each of the tales. Does it seem abrupt and frustrating? Is it a thematic link in the novel? Each time, whether he knows it or not, is it a reprieve . . . for him and the reader?

33. What is suggested by the title? When does Zits dream he is flying? Has he actually flown in planes? Do his characters fly? Is some of his flight away from loneliness and ennui a flight into himself?

34. What separates the story of Jimmy from earlier exploits? How does Zits describe Jimmy? Why does he move into talking about Jimmy in the third person? Why is Abbad a fleeting, in-and-out ghost of a character? How does Jimmy himself fit into the traitor theme? Who have other traitors been in the novel?

35. What did you make of the last time-travel tale, about the drunk homeless Indian? How does he persuade a passerby to show him respect? Is it an ancient mariner story in a way, with someone compelled to tell a story to a stranger? What fundamental mystery of his life has Zits resolved by the end of Chapter 17?

36. Do you think that as a result of all this interpretation of memories the narrator might have a chance of breaking the pattern of three or more generations of alcohol and physical abuse that has pervaded his family?

37. Does Chapter 19, his awakening back in the bank, make you think of the story set in the Civil War, "An Occurrence at Owl Creek Bridge"? (That is a story about a soldier awaiting hanging who dreams a rich escape in his last moments.) Here, Zits says "I have returned to my body. And my ugly face. And my anger. And my loneliness. And then I think, Maybe I never left my body at all. . . . Maybe I've been standing here for hours, minutes, seconds, trying to decide what I should do" (p. 158). What happens next? Is it a new empathy he has for this crowd of attractive, mostly white people? "Maybe we're all lonely. Maybe some of them also hurtle through time and see war, war, war. Maybe

we're all in this together. I turn around and walk out of the bank" (p. 158).

38. How does the story of Auntie Z and her boyfriend determine Zits's character up to the age of fifteen? He's age six and the pattern starts. "Don't tell anybody. Everybody knows you're a liar. Nobody loves you anymore . . . I learned how to stop crying. I learned how to hide inside myself. I learned how to be somebody else. I learned how to be cold and numb" (p. 160-61). Are there multiple battlefields for children?

39. What is significant about Zits's approaching Officer Dave and his partner in the diner? "I want to tell him the entire story. I want to tell him that I fell through time and have only now returned" (p. 162). What is this power of narrative? Does narrative relieve or release the teller? Is it meant to instruct? To form a connection? What does Zits offer to Dave besides the pistols? "Officer Dave . . . I want you to know that I respect you" (p. 163). Is it possible that offering respect is as important as receiving it?

40. At the station house Zits's story about where he got the two guns—from a kid named Justice—is viewed skeptically. "He thinks I invented Justice" (p. 165). Where does that leave you thinking about the whole book? Do you think *Flight* is a fable? Science fiction? Does it matter? What happens on the bank video to leave you wondering?

41. How does Dave's terrible tale in Chapter 20 break down barriers between him and Zits? "Dave weeps. I weep with him" (p. 172).

42. "After months of counseling, social work, mental therapy, and absolute boredom, the medical professionals and social workers and cops decide that I am not going to kill anybody" (p. 173). After his travels into repeated vio-

lence . . . and his own revulsion . . . Zits has to see the irony. Then does he suddenly seem like a healthy, aggrandizing teenager? "I mean, jeez, I'm a fifteen-year-old foster kid with a history of fire setting, time traveling, body shifting, and mass-murder contemplation. I think I might be unlovable" (p. 173). Do you hear what we have learned to appreciate in Zits, that wry humor?

43. Do you find it credible that this angry, insolent street kid can clean up, sit down to breakfast, get his head tousled and say "Wow . . . permanent might be pretty cool"? Has Zits really been transformed to the point of trading "Whatever" for "Wow" with Mary? About Dave, he says, "He's trying to save me. And he's smiling about it. I guess that's okay. Maybe I can save him, too" (p. 177). How is the notion of salvation pursued in Mary's ministering to his acne? "A few months from now, you'll be brand-new" (p. 180). How does this scene compare to the other moment in his time travels when he felt the warmth of family? What are the big differences?

44. What do you think are the chances for success for the renamed boy? "Call me Michael" (p. 181). Is he, after his travel education, ripe for redemption? He has worried over his need to connect with his Indian heritage, but at the end he settles in gratefully with a white family. What do you think this resolution means?

SUGGESTIONS FOR FURTHER READING:

Slaughterhouse-Five by Kurt Vonnegut; *Almanac of the Dead* by Leslie Marmon Silko; *Carrie* by Stephen King; *Bury My Heart at Wounded Knee* by Dee Brown; *In the Spirit of Crazy Horse* by Peter Matthiessen; *102 Minutes* by Kevin Flynn and Jim Dwyer; *The Looming Tower* by Lawrence Wright; *The New Centurions* by Joseph Wambaugh; *The Owl's Song* by Janet Campbell Hale